Alice Valery could not help blushing, the belt of her bathrobe fell undone, and the folds of the garment yawned to show her magnificently buxom body in the scanty dishabille of bra and girdle.

Benito Labirma's eyes widened, and his mouth opened in a kind of sensual awe. He was still a virgin, but that was not to say he did not have demons of desire haunting him in the silence of the night in his little boarding-house room. Yet because he was chaste and pious, and because his parents had brought him up to be humble and self-effacing, he quickly averted his gaze.

Masquerade Books

PASSION
IN
RIO

ANONYMOUS

MASQUERADE BOOKS, INC.
801 SECOND AVENUE
NEW YORK, N.Y. 10017

Reprinted by permission of C.J. Scheiner
Copyright © 1991 by Masquerade Books, Inc.
All Rights Reserved

No part of this book may be reproduced, stored in a retrieval system, or transmitted in any form, by any means, including mechanical, electronic, photocopying, recording or otherwise, without prior written permission of the publishers.

First Masquerade Edition 1991

First printing January 1991

ISBN 1-878320-54-8

Manufactured in the United States of America
Published by Masquerade Books, Inc.
801 Second Avenue
New York, N.Y. 10017

-1-

"This year," said Matteo Borgas, as he dipped his spoon into the heaping bowl his comely young wife, Luisa, had just placed before him, "our *escola* must win the most prizes. Do you understand, woman? Even if it means that I must sell your favors to some rich *gringo turista*, our *escola* from Corcovado must be the very best of all."

Matteo Borgas spoke with passion, for it was two weeks before Rio de Janeiro's great Carnival of '60 would begin. The Carnival is the gala apotheosis of Rio, the greatest folk spectacle in the world, lasting from the Saturday preceding Ash Wednesday until Wednesday evening. Even in the city of Sao Paulo, 250 miles away, lights have to be dimmed, though that city has a Carnival of its own, because Rio draws off so much electrical power for its fabulous ninety-six hours of colorful and riotous merriment.

Luisa Borgas was twenty-two, with lustrous black hair woven in a thick braid that reached the middle of her back. Her face was oval and she had enormous liquid brown eyes, soft satiny skin the color of coffee with milk, sparkling white teeth and a full, sensual red mouth.

Matteo knew that mouth well, as he knew the secret mouth between her round thighs. Both were voracious and could drain him of his manhood. It was a challenge and joy for him to replenish himself quickly, so that he might service his young wife again and again.

Matteo Borgas considered himself one of the lucky ones. He and his young wife lived in a *favela* just behind the mountain of Corcovado, on which stands the world-renowned concrete statue of Christ of the Andes. He was a porter at one of the elegant hotels on the magnificent beach, and he earned considerably better wages than most of his friends and neighbors in this little village built on the side of the huge hill the tourist guides call a mountain. Was he not a *Carioca*, a native of Rio? And was Rio not one of the most gloriously beautiful cities in all the world, a toy set in a misty veil of spun sugar? Here, the ocean, beaches and mountains made up a kind of celestial fairyland. And there was food that even the *porteno* of Buenos Aires could not boast of: the *carambola*, a waxy yellow fruit of indescribable flavor; the *fruta de conde*, or custard apple; the small fragrant cucumber, which one ate boiled, known as the *mixixe*; and this tasty and nourishing *feijoada* that Luisa had just served him.

His wife's lovely brown eyes had widened at his last comment, and she had blushed and then turned away to bring his yerba mate, the herb tea derived from holly served in a hollowed out gourd that was dried and then trimmed with silver. Even the poorest family had its gourd and silver drinking straw for this national beverage.

Again Matteo dipped his spoon into the bowl, savoring the concoction of dark beans cooked with nuggets of meat, sausage and bacon, and seasoned with onions and tomatoes, a dusting of manioc on the top and slices of oranges on the side. No one in all his *favela* could make *feijoada* like his Luisa—nor love, either. He felt his loins throb with memory and desire. Suddenly he wanted her. He took a sip of his *yerba mate*, rose from the table and

Passion In Rio

went back into the crowded little house. She wore a loose blouse and a widely flaring cotton skirt, and there were brass anklets around her slim ankles above her bare feet. He felt his manhood rise in his trousers, and he suddenly reached out his hands and slipped them against her armpits, then vigorously reached forward and down to clutch the pear-like firm globes of her young breasts. Her skin was creamy under his calloused hands. She was as soft as butter and his hot ramrod melted into the crease between her round bottom-cheeks.

He had seen the rich turista women at the Hotel del Lorca, where he worked, wearing their brassieres and their lace-trimmed panties. Some of them were shameless, these *norteamericanos*, because when a bellboy or a porter came into a room, they did not even care that they were in their underclothes and would go on chattering away like parrots to their men while he and his colleagues brought in drink or food.

But Luisa did not need those fancy garments to hide the delectable shape of her young body. Besides, if she had such needless things, he would certainly try to sell them now to one of his neighbors in the *favela*, to raise money for the Carnival. This year it must be something spectacular, beyond belief. Because the merchants and the civic groups would give very large prizes this year, and money too. Many thousands of *cruzeiros*. And if he was lucky enough, and his *escola* won the big prize, why, who knows, he might win enough himself to treat Luisa to a day and a night in a room at a hotel like the Copacabana Palace.

"What are you doing?" Luisa giggled, stiffening but not turning her head as she felt his fingers close over her breasts. At once her nipples began to tingle and to grow flinty with desire. The sensation escalated as he began to roll them between his thumbs and forefingers.

She knew very well what Matteo wanted. Her husband was a young bull, only twenty-six, tireless and insatiable. Not only did he have the stamina of a bull, but a cock that would be the envy of any steer as well. She had been afraid that he would choose instead that scrawny Estella Quemondo, who had not been a virgin at all—like she herself had been. But fortune had smiled upon her, and now there was no need to worry about Estella.

Yes, Luisa Borgas thought to herself as she closed her eyes and let her body go limp and passive against her husband's, she had been a good girl. Oh, well, perhaps at the last Carnival, she had let Jorge Pinson very nearly put his big hard bone into her furry little nest. But at the last moment, in spite of all the *vashaca* she had drunk and the excitement of the Carnival, she had told herself that she must win Matteo and that she would have a better chance if she gave him her flower of virginity.

It had been like making a prayer to the Virgin Sanctissima. By not giving herself to Jorge, she had won Matteo and now that they were married, she could enjoy the pleasure of fucking as often as she wished. She felt his hands tighten against her bosom, and her loins were on fire: It was hard to breathe and she let her head fall back as she closed her eyes and moaned a little, "Me amor, take me…take me…quickly, hard!"

"But not here, *querida*," he muttered thickly, as his hands slid down from her breasts to the smooth goblet of her belly and then went foraging for that other hungry and more secret mouth which was placed between her round satiny thighs. He felt his prick throb with savage vigor against the fly of his trousers, and pressed himself against her lusciously curved, resilient buttocks while the tips of his fingers stroked her pussy through the skirt and the thin cotton of her panties, which she wore beneath. He felt the dampness of her loins as he pressed his fingers through the cotton into Luisa's love hole. Her back stiffened against his sculptured chest as she imagined the delights to come.

It was good to be alive and to be a *Carioca* and to have a woman like Luisa, thought Matteo. And it was better still that this was Sunday, when he did not have to work at the Hotel del Lorca. Because if he'd had to work today, he would be running errands for all those insolent and impossibly rich turista women, flaunting themselves, parading about in their rooms half-clothed, treating him as if he were nothing more than a piece of furniture standing there humbly to pay them homage and yet not able to do anything about their desirable charms. That was the curse sometimes of being young and vigorous, of being a veritable bull or a stallion—as his own sweet Luisa had often called him when they lay together and his prick was buried to the hairs inside that tight hot cavern of hers. It was difficult indeed to keep from showing these insolent bitches who came to visit his beloved Rio that he was perhaps better than any man they had ever had. It would be cause for immediate discharge if any one of them should see the fly of his liveried trousers bulge with desire and report him to old, cranky Esteban Campos, the assistant manager of the Hotel del Lorca whom every porter, bellboy and maid justly feared. That old crow would probably stay away from the Carnival because he regarded pleasure and laughter and music as so much nonsense, the old fool. Just the same, you had to bow your head and do your work and make sure there were no complaints or old Esteban would beckon to you with his bony forefinger and tell you that your days were done.

For a moment he closed his eyes, while Luisa anxiously awaited his pleasure. He was pretending at this moment, this late afternoon of this second Sunday before the great Carnival, that one of the elegantly beautiful *turistas* had called him to her room on some pretext or other, because she could not sleep. And that all she wore was a thin robe through which he could vaguely see the dark patch of private hair at the apex of her thighs. She would be in high-heeled pumps, glossy and glistening, and as she would move about restlessly, he would see the muscles flex in her long calves and thighs. She would have golden hair, a true, and her skin would be pale and delicate like the petals of a white rose. And her eyes would lower to see the bulge in his trousers and she would lick her lips and blush and look away, only to look back once again.

But he would know that she lusted for him, and he would stand there swaggeringly in his manhood, not afraid of old Esteban this time because this *gringa* was hot with wanting him, hot for being plowed like a wheat field by the prongs that dug up the rich soil for the seed that would be planted.

Caught up in his fantasy, his fingers slid to the hips of his wife, and Luisa moaned and bowed her head. Trapped in the narrow little kitchen, yet excitedly awaiting his caprice, Luisa felt all her nerves in flux, all her flesh moist and warm and yearning for the finality of his embrace. As for Luisa herself, though she had to admit that she was often attracted by some of the strong *Carioca* men in the community where they dwelt, there was no one like Matteo who could make her die of passion even before he put his great hard prick deep into her soft squirming cunt.

Matteo's face was hot and darkened with the onrushing blood of rut as he lingered in his little world of fantasy, and the feeling of his young wife's hips against his fingers as he kept his eyes closed and his swollen prick throbbing against the cleft of her ass made the lascivious images rise into his brain still more sharply and violently. Now the lovely rich *gringa rubia* had turned back, her face scarlet, her lips moist and parted, and he could see her breasts rise and fall with an erratic swell. And then she would stammer in an unsteady voice, "B-boy, it's so terribly warm here. Isn't the air conditioning working? Perhaps you could open one of these windows for me and let in a little breeze please." And he would know that she was frantic with her mounting passion and yet too scared—because she was such an untouchably insolent and wealthy turista—to come right out and tell him she what she wanted. And even though her pussy was burning and getting moist with the need of a good stiff prick, she still looked upon him as a menial, as the lowliest of servants, who could not possibly have any meaning for her except as an instrument of service. Yet was this not service which she needed, and did he not have a more than adequate instrument to procure it for her?

"Me Amor," Luisa whimpered as she squirmed against him, rubbing her behind shamelessly against the straining prong that threatened to burst through the stuff of his trousers fly, "why do you keep me waiting? Take me, or for the love of Heaven do it here, because I need you. I want you inside me!"

"Be silent, woman," he gasped out, feeling the hot juices of his rod swell in him like a menacing tidal wave. "I will take you when it pleases me and not before. You are my woman, it is a woman's duty to wait till her husband has need of her, *comprende*? Besides," this with a knowing little chuckle, as his fingers slid back to her belly and then down to tickle her cunt through the thin skirt and panties, "you know very well that the more I play with you, the more exciting it is when you feel my prong between those soft pink lips of yours. I want to feel you and to caress you and to make you die of passion before you even taste what my prick can do for your cunt, Luisa!"

Luisa Borgas bowed her head against her left arm, which pressed against the wall of the little kitchen, and her right hand was at her side, clenched, the nails digging into her moist palm. Waves of lascivious yearning bubbled in her loins, and she felt her cunt churning for her husband's manhood. But like the docile and obedient spouse she was, she did not think of disobeying his injunction. She knew how the other women of the *favela* stared at him as he went jauntily off to work in his fine uniform. Yes, even though they had their own husbands, they wanted what he had between his strong hairy thighs. But it was she, Luisa, who had proprietary rights to that instrument which could draw from her vibrations and emanations such as a skilled musician draws from a tuned harp: rich harmonies and gloriously dark chromatic nuances which transformed her from mere flesh into a pulsating and uninhibited courtesan. Yes, with Matteo she felt as if she could outdo the most passionate lovers of all time, for he was like a god in his loins and fingers and lips and tongue and he could rouse her to incomparable delights which incited her to grant him even more than any woman could give her man.

Shamelessly now, she even wished that he might take her as she was, with his prick gouging against the dainty, puckering crevice of her bottomhole. He had done that only once or twice to her, out of a sudden whim, perhaps because he had been angered by the contemptuous way some rich *gringa* at the hotel had treated him and had pretended he was taking his revenge. It had hurt, those times, but it had been thrilling too, to know herself powerless in his embrace, to know that every orifice in her body could be ravished by that great prick of his and give him pleasure. And besides, it wasn't as if he was simply a selfish animal who used her—no, not Matteo Borgas. For even when she had cried and begged him not to go so fiercely inside that narrower

Passion In Rio

hole, he had reached between her legs with his forefinger and entered the moist pulpy fig of her cunt and began to tickle the little button there until she nearly fainted dead away with ecstasy.

And even as her hips began to salaciously move back and forth with a lingering and provocative enticement to make him take her then and there, Matteo kept his eyes closed and willed himself back in that luxurious hotel room with that *gringa rubia* who could no longer suppress her need for what he could give her. *Diablo*, he had understood very well what she had meant by opening the window. What she wanted was for him to open the lips of that pink slit she had between those long insolent thighs and to fuck her, to treat her like a *puta* and make her forget for one blinding moment that she was one of those untouchable turistas. She would probably have an old, fat and impotent husband with much money and no way to give her pleasure except to buy her pretty things and to bring her to Rio. And that husband would be off at the beach drowsing under the sun, wanting to get his flaccid body tanned and to look young and vigorous again, so that perhaps he could pleasure his wife because she would treat him, too, as contemptuously as she had been treating him, Matteo Borgas.

So he would go to the window with his eyes deferentially lowered, and he would bend his strong back and tug and the window would slide up effortlessly, and this would show the turista how vigorous he was. And then he would turn to her with a contemptuous little smile as if to say, "You see, *senhora*, it was really nothing." And she would utter a little moan and suddenly fling her arms around him and whisper, almost incoherently, "Oh my God, man, don't keep me waiting anymore! Don't you know what I really want? Do it to me, rip off my robe and make me your whore!"

The veins were standing out on his temples, and his body was shuddering from his imagined ecstasies even as his fingers, more urgently now, began to tickle Luisa's pussy. He could feel those plump soft lips twitching and growing moist under his sly dalliance. And he could hear Luisa's little whimpering moans, which told him that she was dying to be fucked. Just as his fantasy *gringa rubia* was longing for his stiff tool. For he would strip away that fine robe of hers and she would be naked, in those gleaming pumps, naked with that pale white skin of the gringa which was like that of a marble statue and unsullied and untouched and unloved because she had been too proud until now to let herself be loved even by her own *esposo*.

He would see the dark-gold curls, crisp and neat in the exquisite triangle which marked her cunt. His hands would close over those pointed, haughty *tetas* of hers, and his nails would score the pale white skin until she winced and groaned. Her knees would be trembling and she would be about to collapse, and yet her arms would hesitantly clasp him about the waist, her head would fall back and her eyes would close, as if even in this moment of renunciation of all her imperious and vaunted chastity, she could no longer hold herself back from this mating.

And then he would fling her down upon the thickly carpeted floor of her hotel room, with a triumphant and sensual laugh, open his fly and let his prick emerge even to the *cojones*, those big hairy balls so full of good hot bubbling seed. At the last moment, her muscular thighs, so long and sleek and white, would tighten as if she now feared that which she so eagerly sought. But it would not deter him. He would knee her thighs apart, his hands still clutching her *tetas* and his mouth would clamp down on hers and brutally silence her plaint. And then the head of his stiff cock would thrust against the

Passion In Rio

silky golden curls of her cunt, force the lips apart and with the roar of a victorious lion he would cram himself up to the hilt inside. How she would writhe and cry out and twist and groan under him, her eyes huge and glassy with mingled fear and lust!

"Tell me how badly you want it, *senhora*," he would gasp, as he rode her. "Beg for it, you shameless gringa *puta*. You've forgotten your husband now, my fine lady, haven't you? You've forgotten that I, Matteo Borgas, am nothing but a servant here to wait upon you head and foot and not to dare to raise my eyes even to your knees. You're feeling what you've raised now though, aren't you, my fine lady? Tell me you're hot for my prick. Beg for it, I want to hear you beg!"

And she would be conquered, and her arms would wrap round him and so would those long white thighs, as she would gasp out. "Oh, God, yes, it's true, fuck me, make me come, screw me, give it to me good, I need it, oh, my God, Matteo, what a man you are!"

His breath was snorting now through his nostrils as the dream became ferocious reality. He twisted Luisa about to face him and now his hands grasped the cheeks of her bottom and he lifted her up in the air as she was spreading her legs and wrapping them nimbly around his strong broad back. He carried her thus, with her hands gripping his strong neck and her eyes glassy with the same desire that the *gringa rubia* would have, as he carried her to their bed. And even as he laid her down, Luisa's slim fingers were tugging up her skirt, and then she was arching up her hips so that he could whisk off the little cotton panties. He didn't even bother to take off his clothes. His fly was already open and his enormous ramrod shudderingly thrust forth in the quest for his young wife's rapacious cunt. With a single lunge, he entered the moist citadel and the greedy lips of her box absorbed and clung to the grisly shaft that pierced her innermost channel. A wailing sob escaped Luisa as her arms and legs locked around her husband, and she gave him her mouth, her tongue lashing between his lips in an implacable demand that at last dispersed the haunting world of fantasy and brought him back into this shuddering and straining present. His hips jerked back and forth as his massive instrument plunged in and out of his young wife's vaginal sheath, shoving itself each time until their hair ground together. He rode her deep and long. It was the kind of fucking Luisa knew she would get when she married Matteo. With her legs wrapped around his waist, she pulled herself up in order for her mouth to meet his; for her tits to be rubbed against his; and for her hole to meet the base of his cock on every thrust. She longed for his joyrod, as much as he wanted to put it to her. As she pulled herself up, Matteo kneaded her ass. This manhandling drove Luisa to the brink. She bit his neck in her transports, her nails gouging his shoulders, and bare legs flexed and now clutched his thighs as she arched herself to absorb their simultaneous joy; hoarse cries of rapture announced the supreme paroxysm.

"*Caramba*," he breathed when it was done at last. "For a piece like you, my little fiery *Carioca*, a rich *turista* would pay many thousands of *cruzeiros*! Just for one time like this, you could earn enough to pay the entire cost of the float which our *escola* is going to enter in the great Carnival!"

-2-

On the fifth floor of the Hotel Metropole, which stood a few hundred yards away from the hotel in which Matteo Borgas worked, a young bellboy was setting down half a dozen gleaming new suitcases just inside the living room of a suite. His name was Renaldo Vaneiros, he was about to celebrate his twentieth birthday on the first day of the great Carnival, and he was enviously eyeing the superb young red-haired woman who was to occupy this elegant set of rooms with her norteamericano husband.

The husband was Roger Porter, an New York advertising man of thirty-seven, and he was thoroughly disgusted over the long, trying flight, which had been somewhat rocky because of turbulence. His disposition was usually sour, and the episode had not sweetened it at all. Moreover, he glumly wished that he had not yielded to Lucille's pleas that before the two of them ended their six-year-old marriage in divorce, they try a second honeymoon.

Lucille Porter was twenty-nine, about five feet seven inches in height with a willowy body. She had elegant long legs, with rather slender thighs, and a provocative, oval-cheeked behind whose undulations along Fifth Avenue invariably drew wolf whistles. And by contrast with her slenderness, she had a pair of magnificent breasts, high-perched, like ripe young cantaloupes, set very closely together, with dark coral nipples set in wide brownish-orangeish aureole. Her coppery-red hair was arranged in a stylish bob, with a sophisticated oval, marked by a delicate aquiline nose with very thin and sensuous wings. Her mouth was rather large, and the lips were thin. Yet the angularity of her cheek-bones and the cat-like luster of her gray-green eyes suggested a smoldering temperament—which she indeed possessed.

Lucille Porter was that curiosity among women, a feverish, almost neurotic beauty who desperately yearned to be possessed and to experience the glorious, shattering earthquake of orgasm, yet who remained frigid even in the midst of her husband's most ardent lovemaking.

She had met Roger Porter at a cocktail party given by the Madison Avenue agency where he was an account executive, because her best girlfriend, who happened to be the mistress of one of his associates, had insisted on bringing her. Lucille Kent, as she had been then, was a frustrated virgin of nearly twenty-one, and she had gone so far as to experiment in lesbian union with Clarissa, her brunette girlfriend and an extremely worldly and knowing amorist. But even that hadn't worked.

Lucille's parents had died when she was only seven, and she had been brought up by her mother's older sister, a retired schoolteacher who frowned with great disapproval on the permissiveness of youth and, more especially, on its freewheeling attitude towards sexual relationships. She believed that marriage was for procreation only, and she had instilled this doctrine in her niece with so many graphic illustrations of the moral depravities and physical suffering that followed yielding to the lustful desire for gratification that the adolescent redhead had been actually terrified of sex. She had managed to keep Lucille from having any dates at all during high school, and by the time Lucille reached college, she herself dreaded the male.

Yet at the same time, because she was a normal, healthy young woman, her body demanded release from the tensions of everyday life, including the pressures of her studies where she sought to reach a high scholastic plateau. So she had resorted to the furtive practice of masturbating while in bed at night; conjuring up erotic fantasies in which some tender and romantic male would be lying beside her caressing her in this dainty and secret nook of her voluptuous young body.

Then and only then could she achieve orgasm. Clarissa had used a dildo on her in that one violent experiment, and Lucille herself had pleaded with Clarissa to initiate her. Up until then, the lovemaking between the two was a much more gentle affair that consisted mostly of stimulating their respective orifices by means of hands, tongues and general contact with one another. It was a generally sweet affair between two women who knew best how to please each other. Yet Lucille needed that something extra; that penile penetration. Having read all the sex manuals, she was morbidly afraid of the shock and brutality of defloration, and she had fallen in love with Roger Porter at their first meeting. Indeed, in her frequent erotic rituals, his face had super-imposed itself over all others in her wildest dreams. And she naively believed that if she could only dispense with the terror of her hymeneal sacrifice, he could come to her and initiate her with the tenderness and the poetry and the beauty that she hoped sexual union would bring because of their love.

Clarissa was a switch-hitter and extremely passionate and uninhibited. She had gone about the defloration gently, first teasing and tantalizing Lucille with her tongue until the lovely young redhead was almost at the point of climax. Then, after anointing the tender spot and the rubber shaft of the artificial phallus as well with a lubricant, she had strapped on the device, taken Lucille in her arms and, reassuring her friend with many kisses and caresses, begun the operation.

Lucille had nearly fainted from the pain, but it was mostly psychosomatic. However, after it was over, she believed that the final barrier to her union with Roger Porter had been eliminated. She was dreadfully wrong.

Roger Porter was a sophisticated New Yorker who had had his first sexual experience at the age of fourteen, and he had a highly egotistical belief in his own amatory powers. Oddly enough, for all his ability, he had not hit upon the idea of oral sex with Lucille—and this might well have saved their marriage. For each time he thrust his virile prick inside her tender cunt, the beautiful redhead seemed to remember the painful laceration caused by Clarissa's dildo, and immediately her muscles tightened and she began to resist. The result was inevitably that she was left hanging in that agonizing abyss while he went on to void his bubbling jism. And gradually a repugnance against her own husband was built up so that when he touched her, she shrank and grimaced.

And yet, contrarily, she loved him more desperately than ever. As for Roger Porter, he had already found himself a much more competent bed partner back in New York, and had been on the verge of asking Lucille to divorce him so that he could remarry. It had been she who, perhaps anticipating his feelings, had pleaded with him for a final chance…a second honeymoon in the most beautiful city in all the world, Rio de Janeiro. If they could only go there during the wonderful Carnival, about which she had read so much, she had told him, perhaps in this exotic city amid all that color and music and gaiety and the happy-go-lucky people who inhabited it, she could find the release from the psychic block-

Passion In Rio

ade which was preventing their union. "Because, you see, Roger darling," she had sobbed, as she knelt before him and looked pitifully up at his stern, handsome face, "it would be different if I didn't love you. But, my God, you don't know what I've been going through. I want you so much. I want to be fucked—yes, darling, I do. And yet I can't seem to get over the terrible things Aunt Lydia used to tell me. If only I could bury her ghost forever—maybe in Rio, you can help me do it and then I'll be the wife you've always wanted me to be. Because for me, Roger you're the man I want to fuck me if anyone ever does."

And because of this direct candor, this pathetically sincere appeal, Roger Porter had grudgingly consented to come to Rio with his wife for the great Carnival.

"The three blue suitcases in the bedroom, if you please, boy," he said to Renaldo.

"*Si, senhor.*" The young *Carioca* deferentially inclined his sleek black-haired head, picked up one of the heavy blue suitcases in each hand and strode into the bedroom of the suite. Lucille Porter smiled at her husband. "We made it, didn't we, Roger darling?" she murmured. "What a beautiful view of the ocean and the mountains! And what glorious sunshine! It'll work out, you'll see. Oh, I want you so, I want you so terribly!"

"Wait till he gets out of here, for God's sake," Roger Porter irritably hissed. He went over to the bay window and lit a cigarette, staring moodily out onto the blue Atlantic, at the incomparable stretch of white sandy beach. He could see the umbrellas of the tourist visitors, and he could also see the strong, supple, glistening, sun-bronzed and almost naked bodies of the women of Rio, in their brief bikinis. Many of them were the mistresses of the wealthy *Cariocas* and would spend a weekend at this or that elegant hotel along the world-famed beach.

He felt his pulses stirring as he saw a laughing black-haired young woman scramble to her feet and run towards the water, a plump bald-headed man in a ridiculously short pair of bathing trunks pursuing her. She was like a pagan nymph out of the jungle, he thought, with her long black hair floating almost to her hips. He could almost see the jouncing globes of full young breasts which strained in the brief bra of her bikini. Desire rose in him. Well, let Lucille indulge her little dream. He'd go along with it. But there must be in this fabulous city so many gorgeous pieces of pussy that even if it didn't work out with her, he could work off his rut all he liked. And, damnit, he would! There weren't many men who would put up with a neurotic bitch like Lucille. Sure, she was intelligent, witty, dressed beautifully, cooked marvelously, and she had a delicious figure. He still wanted her, but was it asking too much for man a to fuck a girl for six years and just once bring her to a gushing climax, to feel her clawing and biting and scratching and locking her arms and legs around him and sinking her teeth in his shoulder in the final rapturous fury of orgasm? Now with one of those brown-skinned, full-bosomed Brazilian girls he'd seen in the travel folders and magazines, he could probably go off a dozen times a night.

The handsome young bellboy came back to take up the last blue suitcase and put it in the bedroom, and then smiled at the grumpy norteamericano. "And these, *Senhor*?" he asked in a soft voice, in excellent English given fascinating nuances by his Portuguese accent, as he gestures towards the three gray suitcases.

"I'll take care of them. Thanks." Roger Porter took out his wallet and handed the youth a bank note. "You're a polite enough fellow. Are you the regular bellboy for us here?"

"I can arrange to be, *Senhor*," Renaldo said with a dazzling smile, though it was directed at the red-haired

Senhora. "I have but to tell Porfirio—that is our bell captain, *Senhor*—that whenever you wish service, I, Renaldo Vaneiros, am to be sent to serve you."

"That's fine, you do that. Oh say, one thing more. This big Carnival of yours, can we foreigners take part in it?"

"But of course, *Senhor*. There are many places where you and your lovely *esposa* may go to dance. Or then again, if the *Senhor* and his *esposa* wish, they may wear costumes and go out into the streets with the *Cariocas*. The Carnival welcomes all, rich or poor, for it is our time of joy before the fasting and solemnity of Lent."

"How charmingly he speaks our language, Roger," Lucille Porter exclaimed. "If everyone is as nice in Rio as this young man, it's going to be a wonderful time for us, don't you agree?"

"The *Senhora* is too kind," Renaldo said modestly, again showing his strong white teeth in a dazzling smile which this time was turned full in her direction, much to Roger Porter's annoyance. "I have learned English at the school, because one day, if I am fortunate, I hope to visit your beautiful country and perhaps to even work there at one of the hotels."

"With manners like yours, I'm sure you'll be very welcome, especially in New York," Lucille Porter laughed. Her husband gave her a furious glance at this, and then lit a another cigarette and went back to the window to stare out on the beach. He saw the black-haired nymph come out of the water, saw the fat man catch her by the wrists and draw her to him, saw her struggle and then, throwing back her head with a laugh, clasp him in her arms and kiss him hotly on the mouth. And he felt his prick swelling in savage frustration. Damn it, if that little bitch were only here right now, how he'd fling her on the bed and give it to her. How he'd like to do that with Lucille, but it wouldn't work.

Nothing worked. She was as frigid as a glacier, for all her talk of wanting to be fucked. She was just talking herself into a nervous breakdown, but he was the one who was going to have one if something wasn't done before long. All right, he'd spend two weeks here, and then he'd go back to New York and start divorce proceedings.

His back was turned, and he didn't see how Renaldo Vaneiros had suddenly taken Lucille Porter's hand and kissed it, as he would that of a great lady. Nor did he see that the bellboy's fly was bulging. For this handsome young *Carioca* who longed so to work in a hotel in the United States, longed even more to thrust his prick into the soft cunt of an American girl. Ever since Porfirio had described with lurid details how he, the captain of all these contemptible bellboys, had slept with the rich *Senhora* Donaldson, that blonde with the big *tetas*, he had been wild with envy to find out what it was like. He had his own sweetheart, Eleanora Consalvez, and she was willing enough to go to bed with him whenever he wished. But he was tiring of her now, because his prick had visited her cunt too many times for there to be novelty in it. But with this one, this tall and sweet *turista* with the hair that was the color of fire, now that would be a different story!

-3-

Miguel Valdes, night porter at the famous Trocadero Hotel on beautiful Copacabana Beach, was certain that his young wife Miranda was cuckolding him with Francisco da Rucosta, the handsome and dignified assistant manager of the Trocadero's beautifully decorated and lavish restaurant. He couldn't prove it, but he had a plan. One of the bellboys had told him that Francisco was going to take part in the Carnival as a member of the *escola* of Urca, the group in which he himself was a leading spirit. He would bribe young Pedro to tell him what costume Francisco was going to wear, and he would watch to see how the swine approached his own beautiful Miranda in her Gypsy costume with the imitation gold earrings and the sparkling tiara which was, alas, paste and not the diamonds she deserved. No, she didn't deserve them, come to think of it! Because if he found that Miranda was taking Francisco's prick between those long olive-sheened legs of hers, he would kill them somewhere on Sugar Loaf Mountain.

He chuckled grimly at the fantasy. He would cut off Francisco's prick and stuff it into Miranda's cunt, and bury her in one grave on one side of the mountain and that great lover on the other. And throughout eternity the spirit of Francisco would be wailing through the shadows seeking his lost manhood and never finding it. That would be a fitting end for that gay blade who fancied himself such a *romantico* with the damas.

Miguel Valdes was forty—short and squat, his black hair receding, and just this morning in the mirror in the bathroom he had discovered one or two small bald patches. He was getting a double chin, too, but then nature had never been too kind to him, not as it had been to that bastard Francisco. For Francisco was not yet thirty, and a bachelor to boot, so he had much more liberty to pursue all the sweet cunts who came to the hotel and who sported on the beach in the skimpiest bikinis.

But, apart from the age difference and the good looks of his suspected rival, Miguel Valdes knew perfectly well that he could satisfy Miranda's lusts far better than any young caballero. She came from a poor *favela* back near Sao Paulo, the great industrial city of Brazil. Indeed, her little village had not been far away from the famous Snake Institute Butantan where the turistas came to see the extraction of venom from the fangs of the deadly reptiles. Her father had died about five years ago and her mother had brought her to Rio in the hope of finding her a job as a maid at one of the smaller hotels like the Maraba or the Danubio. But there hadn't been any openings there, and so the old woman had brought delicious Miranda to the Trocadero. It had been just his good luck that *Senhor* Benito Villegas, the hotel manager, had asked him to work days that week instead of nights, so he had been bringing in parcels from the mail truck to the lobby desk when Miranda had been timidly speaking to the fiercely mustachioed, white-haired manager. No, there hadn't been a job for the likes of her. *Senhor* Villegas had indicated as much with a great scowl and much flourishing of his shaggy eyebrows. And he, Miguel Valdes, had seen Miranda begin to cry softly, while her mother drew her away,

Passion In Rio

chiding her angrily for making such a scene in this elegant hotel.

He had deposited his parcels at the desk, said that he was going back for more, and then hastening around from the back of the hotel had gone around to the front just in time to catch the mother and daughter before they went sadly and slowly down the long paved walk towards the other hotels along the beach. He had introduced himself with a very courtly bow and a smile which showed his gold-capped teeth of which he was very proud. Not every night porter could afford such dental work. But he, Miguel Valdes, had earned many large tips because of his very special services to the middle-aged and yet still handsome turista women who stayed at the Trocadero and found themselves longing for a man. Why, only the night before, after he had finished his shift at about three in the morning, the telephone had rung in the little receiving room at the back of the hotel, and when he had picked it up, it had been the *Senhora* Amelia Jenson, that tall and bespectacled but quite good-looking spinster who had come all the way from New York to spend her vacation at the Trocadero.

She had been there two weeks already, and she was going to spend another week or two just because of him, he knew.

As he sat at his desk and took off his cap and leaned back in his chair this evening, he closed his eyes and remembered again the fiery passion of that turista *Senhora*.

She had been there for about a week and all the bell-boys, including Pedro, who always got along with the ladies because he spoke such excellent English, had reported that she was very cold and distant and treated them all like the worst of menials. And then one night, after he had finished his chores, he decided to pretend to be a rich tourist and had put on his bathing trunks which he kept in his locker, and gone out for a stroll along the white sands of the magnificent beach. The air had been soft and gentle, and the water just the right temperature. He had cavorted like a fish, spluttering and puffing and throwing himself this way and that against the gently lapping waves. And when he had emerged, to his great surprise, a woman had been standing there watching him. It had been the *Senhora* Jenson. And she had smiled and spoken in halting Spanish to him, of which he could understand enough, Portuguese-born though he was, to realize that she was praising him for his love of life and wishing that she too could swim and he had told her that he would teach her; did she have a bathing suit? And she had laughed for the first time, showing beautiful strong white teeth, and nodded, and told him that she would go back to her hotel room and bring it out.

Aidime, what a night it had been! Because once she had come out in the bathing suit, he had felt his prick stiffening at the very sight of her. Tall, about five feet eight, with a rather angular face, but one which the moonlight softly shadowed into actual beauty. Big brown eyes, full soft mouth which had no lipstick. Indeed, her skin was much too pale, indicating that she rarely got outdoors. By some standards she might even have been considered homely, for her nose was just a trifle crooked, and her eyelids were rather heavy and the eyes themselves a watery pearl-blue. But her body—that was a different story! Such *tetas*, full and widely spaced, and high-perched on her chest, and what a magnificent behind! Broad full oval-shaped globes, which the bathing suit shaped out even to showing the gradually widening crease. Long beautiful slender thighs and slim girlish calves and all that pale white skin, with a delicious little birthmark, a tiny brown oval patch, high on the

Passion In Rio

inside of her left thigh, almost hidden by the short legs of the one-piece suit.

Well, *Senhora* Jenson hadn't minded that he was paunchy and getting just a little bit bald and had not just bulging calves and thighs but one big bulge between his thighs, in his tight bathing trunks. Not one little bit, she hadn't. They'd sat there talking, and he had spoken enough English to get in a word or two edgewise. She told him a good deal about herself. She was thirty-five and she worked as an office manager in a stenographic pool in a big office in a huge building back in New York City. She'd won about a thousand American dollars in an office pool betting on the Indianapolis auto race, and so she had decided to come to Rio.

Then they had swum together—rather, he taught her how in waist-deep water, holding her body, directing her legs and arms while she giggled like a schoolgirl and blushed at the feel of his pudgy fingers on her bare flesh and on her thinly-sheathed lithe body.

And when the lesson was over, as they were coming back to the sands, she had stumbled and he had caught her, his hand accidentally cupping and flattening one of those gorgeous big round tetas of hers. She had groaned a little, looked at him with widened eyes, then suddenly with a little whimper had put her arms around him and kissed him hotly on the mouth.

He had very nearly taken her then and there, but even at that late hour on the beach there was always danger of discovery. Sometimes the little brats out of the poorer quarters of Rio would steal down to the rich hotel areas and pretend that they, too, were rich turistas, and once in a while the older and bolder ones would blackmail some of the couples who were foolish enough to fuck out there under the moonlight or even beat and rob them.

Fortunately, it hadn't gone quite that far, but just

enough to get *Senhora* Jenson mad to have him. With his hand between her thighs pressing against her cleft, she had whispered, "Miguel, Miguel, I-I've never had a man before—but I want you so—oh God, where can we go, where can we go quickly where you can show me what it's like to be loved? I've never been loved, dear Miguel...will you love me tonight?"

The damnable thing about it was that Miguel couldn't very well take her back to the hotel in the *favela* where he lived, because it might disgust her and put her out of the mood, nor could he very well take her back into the hotel because it would mean his job. But then he recalled that there was a little beach house reserved for the guests of the Trocadero, and with great good luck he found that the old watchman hadn't snapped the padlock tight. So he'd taken Amelia Jenson into one of the stalls and closed the door, and then, before she could get out of the mood again, he'd fondled her breasts and kissed her hard on the mouth while she moaned and clutched at him, her head falling back, her eyes closed, her body shaken by intermittent shudders of desire mingled with a deliciously virginal apprehension.

It hadn't been too pleasant at first because she had a very thick hymen, understandably after not having gotten herself fucked in all these years. But once the pain of it was over, once she began to feel his thick prong prodding away for dear life down deep in that sweet hot cunt of hers, the *Senhora* Jenson had forgotten that she was a dignified spinster and a *norteamericana*, and had clawed at him and bitten him and rolled over and over on the stone floor like an animal in heat. He'd had her three times and she couldn't get enough after that. Almost every night during her stay, there had been a ring for him down in the receiving room which would mean that when he had finished his shift, he'd steal up

Passion In Rio

the back freight elevator up to the fourth floor, then walk up the stairs and tiptoe to her room on the seventh. And she would insist on keeping him there almost till noon the next day, and by then she'd been so frenzied in her lust that he had dared to jeopardize his job.

But of course when he'd met Miranda, everything had changed. Miranda was then twenty, shy, with huge brown eyes, long black hair that fell to her waist and breasts like pears, set closely together and thrusting out their points insolently through her thin blouse. Delicious olive-sheened legs, with rippling thighs whose very muscularity foretold the most insatiable passion between them.

So he had courted her under her mother's very eyes, boasted of his position at the Trocadero, told her of his hoarded wealth. *Senhora* Jenson hadn't been the first *turista* he had fucked and been well paid for doing so. He'd amassed many American dollars, and he had them all in a bank and he had the little book to prove it. He had been smitten by Miranda, and he knew that the only way he could get her was to marry her, so after treating the mother to the best dinner in one of the cheaper restaurants where it didn't matter if you weren't too richly dressed, and with Miranda hanging on his every word, he had made a formal proposal of marriage. The old woman had seen the wisdom of that proposal and given him her blessing.

Well, he and Miranda had been married the following week and there hadn't been any more time for the *Senhora* Jenson, and the latter had gone back to the *Estados Unidos* very unhappy—but still not without leaving him a very generous tip.

And everything he had anticipated about Miranda had come true. Yes, she had been a virgin too, but an impatient one, eager to be rid of the restraint of her hymen. On their wedding night, she had practically raped him in her furious desire to be a woman and to make up for the sheltered vigilance under which her mother had kept her away from all the men who had sniffed at her cunt. And she could bite and scratch and claw, almost strangle him with her arms and legs, and almost break his back with her wild tossing and weaving when she felt his prick reaching that last quickened cadence before the final spasm, and they had four glorious years together. During that time, he recognized how her passion drove her like a lioness. She would often take the lead in their lovemaking, having clambered on top of him in order to straddle his manhood. "Push it up into me," she would command, and he would have no choice to do anything else. She would bend over to place her *tetas* dangerously close to his mouth just to tease him. His tongue would be outstretched and she would pull back. Being angered, Miguel would stuff his cock as deep into her as he could, never realizing that was exactly what Miranda wanted. Yes, she knew how to get what she wanted, and if she went elsewhere to get it, so be it. She hadn't minded until now that he was getting fat and bald and hairier than ever—not as long as he could service her voracious and insatiable cunt when she wanted it.

Only now, and it had been all his own fault, she might well be making eyes at Francisco da Rucosta. Because, like a fool, to celebrate having saved all of twenty-five hundred good American dollars in the bank, he had decided on his day off to dress in his very best, to buy her a new dress, and to take her to the Trocadero's fine restaurant for dinner. That bastard Francisco himself had waited on them and he had made the most elaborate and gallant speeches to Miranda, and it had probably turned her head.

Well, the Carnival wasn't far off now. And as soon as he found out for certain that Francisco and Miranda

Passion In Rio

were deceiving him behind his back, he'd know what to do. Because in the crowds and in the noise and all the excitement of those four wonderful days and nights, you could commit murder and get away with it.

-4-

The Porters were not the only couple from New York City who had come to Rio to enjoy the great Carnival. There were others, and two of them had made reservations at the Hotel Metropole, the very one in which Roger and Lucille Porter were occupying a suite on the fifth floor.

On the floor above, a young bellboy with sleek black hair, the soft brown eyes of a doe and the gentle speech of a villager (Benito Lobirma had come, indeed, from a little *favela* about fifty miles away, and had had great good fortune in being accepted as a member of the hotel's staff) was bringing in the suitcases of two attractive young women, both of whom worked for a fashionable dress designing house in Manhattan. One of them was Kay Arnold, twenty-eight sleek, with an autocratic face, highset cheekbones, gray-green eyes, an insolent small ripe mouth and a sensuous aquiline nose. She was about five feet seven inches in height, beautifully dressed, and she outranked her slightly younger companion, Joanne Claremont, at the Salon of Mathilda.

The Salon of Mathilda had been founded three short years ago by a woman in her early forties who had herself been one of the most fashionably dressed women in New York and had always had an innate ability to design her own clothes. Under the domination of her rich and somewhat sadistic husband, she had never really had the opportunity, to do anything on her own, for

Passion In Rio

he looked upon her efforts to find some worthwhile hobby as a direct insult to him. But when she had found him making love to his male secretary in their Long Island summer house where she had shown up unexpectedly late one afternoon, she had told him that he would either give her a divorce and a handsome settlement, or there would be a scandal the likes of which would destroy him. Grudgingly, he had acceded to her demands. Much to Mathilda's dismay, the scandal ensued nonetheless once the trial began.

When Donald Doran was asked to give testimony, no one was quite sure what he would say—he might even "take the fifth." What they got was a blow-by-blow account of the afternoon.

Doran and his assistant, Michael, had gone to the beach house in order to finish hammering out a deal to be presented to some exporters the following Monday. A summer weekend by the pool might help ease the situation and get them away from the phones.

They had just gotten to the house and settled down in the library to work. The late afternoon sun was blazing through the windows of a house not yet air conditioned. Doran sat at his big mahogany desk, with Michael in the green leather chair facing him. The pair were still in their office attire having started the day there, and because Doran was such a hard-ass about the way his employees looked, ties and jackets were required, even in the dog days of August. But out in Oyster Bay, and with the Mediterranean swarthiness of his assistant facing him, Doran felt an urge for some...informality.

"You might take off your jacket and tie, Michael. I know it's hot as blazes in here."

"Yes, Mr. Doran."

"The windows in here have been stuck shut since of the war of 1812, I think."

Doran noticed a tuft of hair at Michael's throat as he unbuttoned his collar. And furry arms, as the cuffs were rolled up.

"No offense lad, but I see perspiration stains on your shirt. If you don't want those to be permanent, you'd best take it off."

"Thank you, Mr. Doran. Since I got my first paycheck from you last week, I splurged and bought this shirt at Brooks Brothers. I don't want to ruin it."

As he did, Doran saw just how hirsute this man was. And how developed. The pectorals were built up, as were the biceps. An athletic undershirt encapsulated the trim torso like a second skin.

"You have a fine build, son. Do you exercise?"

"I get to the 'Y' on occasion. Is there somewhere I can plug in the electric typewriter to type up the notes?"

"Over here, by the window."

As Michael bent over to plug the machine in, Doran noticed the roundness of his assistant's ass. It was as if a melon was split in half and placed high on the posterior of the young man's frame.

"You know, with your build, you might actually be able to get this window open."

"Let me give it a try."

"Let me give you a hand."

As the boy stretched his arms upward to reach the sash, Doran positioned himself behind him, Michael's elbow in the crook of the older man, back against torso. The younger man heaved, and Doran's cock pushed itself against the fabric clad ass of the young buck.

"Mr. Doran, I...I don't think the window will open. It's...it's very tightly shut.

"As tight as that ass, boy?"

"Please sir, let's get back to work." Michael tried to pass by his boss, but as he did, the older man's hand grabbed his crotch.

Passion In Rio

"Seems like you've got quite a package there, lad. What do you do with something like that?"

"Not...not what you think, sir. Besides which...you're married."

"Yes, but I like to swing on something once in a while."

Doran was standing right next to the chair to which Michael retreated. He was playing with the dark curls when he pushed his worker's face against his hard rod.

"Don't think you'd like to taste that, do you? Well, how about getting another paycheck out of me? Maybe one that's bigger?" Gnashing the boy's mouth against his manstick, he added roughly, "Though not this big."

"Mr. Doran, are you saying that you'll fire me if I...if I don..."

"That's right, boy. So get to it."

Doran sat down on the burgundy couch, unbuttoned his shirt (but left his tie on), unzipped his pants and pulled out his prick. Starting to jerk it off, he turned to his young employee and commanded him: "Get down on it."

Michael thought it over but realized that this job was very important right now. Reluctantly, he knelt before his boss and tentatively started to lick the man's organ.

"Not like that, boy. Haven't you ever sucked a cock before?"

"No."

"No, what?"

"No, sir."

"That's better, son. Gently in and out, like you're sucking a lollipop. But watch the teeth!"

Michael started again, and got appreciatively better, Doran thought. The businessman reach over the cocksucker and started massaging the boy's ass.

"Feels like that ass is ripe to get opened wide, doesn't it, boy?"

Michael stopped sucking long enough to gasp with astonishment at the older man's suggestion. Certainly, it was not the first time he had imagined such things. Michael's thoughts turned feverishly back to the many fantasies he'd harbored as a young boy of just such an encounter. How he had imagined it would feel to have his most private orifice filled by the cock of an older man, a stronger man, a man who would not take no for an answer. But like this? With a man such as Mr. Doran? No, it was too terrible—and too exciting.

Doran's voice interrupted his reverie.

"I said, it feels like that ass is ripe to get opened. Didn't you hear me, boy? Hasn't anyone come knocking at your back door before, boy?"

Doran laughed, as he continued to knead the boy's round ass cheeks. At that moment, he groaned deeply as Michael's sucking began in earnest at the thought of what Doran had in mind.

"Yes, I see, you are not totally adverse to the idea, are you? Perhaps you even want to feel the full weight of my cock shoved in your little ass." With that, Doran began to pump into Michael's mouth with new ferocity. Groaning, he began to tease Michael's tight orifice with his index finger, winding around it with a light circular motion and then pushing insistently at the resistance of his dark ring.

Michael choked when he felt the intrusion and tried to pull his mouth away from Doran's cock for a brief respite.

"Mr. Doran, please, no! I have never done this before! I cannot! Please, let me satisfy you with my mouth. I can make you come like this. Let me, please!"

Before he could finish, Doran shoved his cock back into the boy's mouth, nearly touching the back of his throat with the swollen knob of his hard shaft. Michael opened his mouth wider to take the full length of

Passion In Rio

Doran's cock down his throat, and resigned himself to the inevitable.

"So you're a virgin are you? All the better. I like virgin assholes, they're so tight and hot on my cock I can hardly keep from coming."

With that, Doran pulled the boy's pants down to his knees in one quick movement. Without pausing, he pushed his finger into the boy's asshole and began a series of thrusting and circling motions designed to prepare the boy for his imminent penetration.

"Do it to me, like this," Doran commanded. "Put your finger in my ass and pull it in and out. Pump it in and out of me like you would fuck a beautiful woman."

Michael obeyed, reaching his hand around to Doran's butt and fumbling between the cheeks until he found the desired portal. Tentatively, and then with increasing boldness, he inserted his finger into the receptive opening. Michael felt the building excitement in his loins. A unique sensation that only occurs when one is performing a new and forbidden act. The combination of fear and desire caused him to increase the speed with which he sucked Doran's cock.

Doran felt his excitement reaching a new plateau. He pulled his cock out of the boy's mouth and swung him around in one commanding movement. He half-dragged, half-lured the boy over to a corner of the room where a small mirror was hanging. Bracing the boy against the adjacent wall, Doran was able to view both of their midsections in the reflection. Grasping him by the hips, Doran maneuvered his cock into the slit between the boy's round, firm ass cheeks.

To his own surprise, Michael found himself melting against the upward thrusting of the older man's cock against his ass. He felt wildly out of control, no longer did he protest or resist Doran's manipulations. Instead he gave in, and felt the release of his inhibitions unleash

39

his own cock from its slumber. It sprang to life, slapping against his stomach and throbbing with anticipation.

Doran reached around and grabbed the newly erect member of the boy. Watching in the mirror, Michael saw the older man begin to pump his thick rod in time with the movement against his backside. Michael moaned with pleasure, there was no turning back now—he had to have it inside him.

Doran's cock slid easily between Michael's cheeks, lubricated from the juices in the boy's mouth. Up and down, in a slow, regular motion, Doran continued his movements, occasionally teasing the twitching ring of the young man's asshole with the purple, engorged head of his penis. Suddenly, he stopped, and grabbed his cock in his hand and aimed it at Michael's quivering hole.

"Are you ready, boy? I have to get inside you now!"

Michael turned again towards the mirror and saw Doran poised at the entrance to his rear. He couldn't take his eyes off the scene of his own seduction. It couldn't believe it was really happening, but it was. Michael reached around and pulled his ass cheeks apart and began moving backwards towards Doran. The tickling sensation he felt in his ass was overcoming him and it mingled with the ache he felt in his cock as Doran continued to squeeze and stroke it.

Without warning, Doran thrust forward and pushed the head of his cock inside the welcoming depths of Michael's virgin hole. Michael cried out in pain as his boss immediately began pushing in and out, without stopping to let Michael adjust to the intrusion. Doran pumped the boy's cock with renewed enthusiasm, and Michael found the distraction stimulating enough to help him to relax and accept the huge shaft that bore inside him.

"Yes...yes...I've wanted this...I wanted to put my cock in your ass since I hired you," Doran gasped. "I've

Passion In Rio

wanted to feel it shooting in...and out...of this tight asshole until I come. Open up, open up and let me fuck your ass. Oh god, I'm so close, I'm going to shoot inside you."

Michael felt his own climax drawing close. Doran continued pumping rapidly in and out of him as he pulled down hard on Michael's rock hard shaft.

Doran began grunting low and deep as he thrust, slower now, into Michael. He drove so deep inside that Michael was sure he'd feel Doran's cock tickling his own stiff weapon. Suddenly, Michael felt a deep shaking begin in his spine and radiate through his legs, up his now glistening torso, and course to the tips of his fingers. He began to buck uncontrollably and as he did, Doran increased the friction of his hand on Michael's cock. A heat flowed through his body and with it, a feeling of total abandon and then, finally, release. Michael watched in the mirror, as his own thick spunk pulsed out of him.

The image of the boy's crisis was too much for the older man. His balls were tight and full, ready to explode the minute he let go for so much as an instant. Without warning—just at the moment of his orgasm—the door to the room came crashing open and Doran turned to face the ashen face of his wife Mathilda.

"Oh...Oh my god. No..." Mathilda reached backward as if to steady herself. Of all the thousands of small betrayals that had troubled their marriage, nothing had prepared her for the sight of her husband's cock pounding in and out of the asshole of his male secretary. Unable to find the words to express her horror, she ran from the room and out of the house forever.

When all was said and done, the stoic wife, Mathilda Doran, walked off with the lion's share of the couple's savings and property.

So with the lump sum given her in the divorce, Mathilda Doran had boldly hired five or six gifted young women, luring them away from established fashion houses with lavish promises of a profit-sharing scheme, which, if she proved successful, would earn them from two to three times as much as they were presently earning. Two of these girls had been Kay Arnold and Joanne Claremont, each from a different fashion house.

Kay Arnold had been married once for six months, at the age of seventeen, but the marriage had been annulled by her parents. Unlike most adolescents who seek freedom, she had actually been grateful to them for having broken up her marriage. For she had discovered that she found sex with a man nauseating and detestable, and on the very day when she had celebrated the annulment, she had gone to bed with a pretty manicurist who worked in the hotel where her parents were living. Since then, she had become a passionate lesbian, to the point that her affairs with models and even buyers were becoming slightly notorious.

Mathilda Doran had sensed this, but she had had no proof, and she had thought it wise to send Kay to Rio to cover the Carnival. Her feeling was that the flamboyant and gaily colored costumes of this great celebration might bring forth some dramatic and boldly original concepts which could be put to realization in her own salon. She had sent Joanne Claremont as Kay's companion because Joanne was very happily engaged to an ambitious young lawyer, David Shelby, and it appeared that nothing could hamper their romance. Indeed, they were to be married as soon as Joanne returned from the Rio assignment. Thus Mathilda Doran thought that with the stabilizing influence of a girl who loved a man sincerely, Kay's wantonness might be kept in check.

She had believed this so thoroughly, indeed, that she

Passion In Rio

had taken Joanne aside and intimated that Kay might be able to use Joanne's clearheaded and friendly guidance. The fact was that Kay's designs were so brilliant that Mathilda Doran was afraid of losing her and was willing to try anything to change the brunette's erotic penchant—one which might bring scandal not only upon herself but on the salon for which she worked.

Kay Arnold was quite well aware of this, and she personally thought Joanne a "square." Joanne Claremont was blonde, delightfully rounded of bosom and hips and thigh, with sky-blue eyes, a gracious, smiling mouth that was made for kisses, dimpled cheeks and a soft sweet voice. Indeed she seemed younger than she actually was, but her beauty was such that Kay lusted for her. And now that they were here in Rio, the world's most beautiful city and practically on the eve of the great Carnival, Kay Arnold was planning how she could overcome Joanne's defenses and convert her to the sweeter, if forbidden, joys of lesbian love.

The other couple from New York was, actually, a trio, for it comprised an attractive widow and her teenaged son and niece—a girl she and her husband had raised since her parents died, years earlier. Mrs. Alice Valery, buxom and brown-haired, would celebrate her fortieth birthday during the week of Carnival, was still mourning her virile and hardworking husband Daniel, who had died of a heart attack three months ago. They had been planning to come to Rio for the Carnival, and because she had loved him dearly and because the two of them had been inseparable in bed, Alice Valery had impulsively decided to go to Rio anyway because it was what Daniel himself would have wished for his family. They might well have stayed at a more luxurious hotel, for Daniel Valery had left his wife a quarter of a million dollars in cash, bonds and securities. But Alice Valery had come from a poor family and her husband himself had been only an assistant chemist in a huge pharmaceutical company when he had stumbled upon a formula for an antiseptic mouthwash while testing for quite a different type of product. He had realized that if he turned the formula over to his employers, he might get a small bonus and nothing more, and so he gambled. He resigned his job and went to the products manager of a rival though smaller firm and made a proposition. Ten years later, he was wealthier than he had ever dreamed he could be. And yet Alice Valery had never really let her husband's unexpected wealth go to her head or in any way change her from the simple and unaffected woman she had always been—which was one reason he had loved her so dearly.

But his hard work and sudden determination to be as wealthy as he could had somehow estranged him from her the last three or four years, and he actually died from overwork. Alice had sorrowed long before his death to see him turn from her and forget their early years of hardship when they had so steadfast a relationship, especially in bed. She felt herself to be a one-man woman, and she gloried in it. She was always ready for him, tired though she might be from bringing up the children and from housework. Whenever he turned to her, and his hand touched her round satiny full thigh, she shuddered and her love juices began to seep into her loveshaath, preparing her well in advance for the sturdy dig of his stiff prick. Even during his deepest preoccupation with his work, Daniel always had time for the woman he married. He delighted in Alice so much that some days he would come home from work during the day, pretending to be one salesman or another and surprise his wife, who would be wearing nothing but a housecoat. "My husband is a very jealous man," she would exclaim.

"I don't give a flying fuck about your husband,"

Passion In Rio

Daniel snorted back, while running his hands between the snaps of his wife's shift. Pushing Alice back in the house, he would take her to the first room he thought of, sometimes the kitchen, and would lift her up on any available surface. He would kneel between her legs as he serviced her pussy with his tongue.

"But the children..." Alice would protest, knowing they wouldn't be home from school for another two hours.

"Yeah, maybe they'll have some brothers or sisters soon," was the answer Daniel invariably gave as he opened his fly and grabbed his stiff prick through the hole in his boxer shorts. He would pull his pants down to his ankles and give it to Alice right there on the kitchen table until their love juices spilled out onto the polished surface. Daniel would scurry back to work, and Alice would understand if he worked late that night.

She mourned him still. She was not certain that she would ever marry again, though even now, seeing the beauty of that beach and the ocean and the mountains, she longed to be with a man like Daniel Valery, who would take her around to see the sights, treat her to the best dinner in town, and then make passionate and thoroughly satisfying love to her in bed. Perhaps here in Rio, in the turbulent excitement of a great fiesta, Alice Valery secretly thought she might, if only for a few hours, find some man who would give her back her womanhood and make her glory in it as Daniel Valery had done until his worship of Mammon had turned him from a lover into an obsessed provider.

Her son, Lawrence, eighteen, sturdy and tall, just over the awkwardness of adolescence, resembled Daniel in as many ways. Phyllis, daughter of her husband's brother, was sixteen, and resembled her husband's family. There was a voluptuous ripeness about her teenaged nubile body, though. Phyllis had dark-brown hair, which she wore it in helmet style. It was somewhat like Alice Valery's, though hers was a more mature coiffure—a tidy oval bun on the back of her head. Phyllis was animated, wildly in love with Elvis Presley and the latest folk and rock groups, and she was beginning to discover that boys were not nearly so obnoxious as she had thought a few years before.

She liked her cousin, though she thought him at times something of a square. She had no way of knowing that Lawrence wanted to fuck her, and had had that desire, as a matter of fact, ever since he had happened to discover a hole in the wall of his closet that connected with her bedroom and saw her taking off her clothes about a year ago. From that time on, many a night he had tossed and turned, unable to sleep, knowing that she was on the other side of the wall, until he could find relief only by closing his eyes, playing with his cock and pretending that her soft little hand was frigging him.

He had been reading a great deal about the Carnival and how rich and poor alike forgot their sorrows and problems for those four exciting days and nights, how, just as in the New Orleans Mardi Gras, one could cast off inhibitions and, by putting on a mask and costume, find adventure and passion and romance. Perhaps, he thought to himself, as soon as his mother had joyously announced her decision to take them all to Rio, he would have a chance to get Phyllis alone and to show her how much he wanted her and how he could make her happy by sticking his stiff aching cock into that dainty dark-brown-fleeced slit of hers.

-5-

Gottfried von Arnheim walked over to the huge bay window that looked down on the magnificent beach of Copacabana, and frowned with the eye of a connoisseur who is accustomed to nothing but the finest. He was dressed in an expensive linen suit, and his shoes were made of white calfskin tooled in Peru. In his pudgy right hand dangled one of his Upmann cigars, which were shipped to him past the Cuban blockade at a cost of over a dollar each.

But money was of little concern to Gottfried von Arnheim, because he had managed to salt away a fortune of nearly two million dollars in a Swiss bank in Zurich just before the sudden collapse of the Third Reich. He had fled to Lisbon just two weeks before the Allies invaded Berlin and the Madman of Munich had killed himself and his beloved Eva Braun in a bunker under the streets.

He was fifty-six, his head was bald and round like a billiard ball, and he had shaved off his characteristic Prussian mustache in a further attempt at disguise, for he was high on the list of wanted Nazi criminals. He had managed to reach first a friendly compatriot in Buenos Aires who had given him a job as a foreman in a soap factory to hide him away for a year or two at the time when the pursuit of Nazi criminals had reached its height, just after the Nuremberg trials. Then he had gone to Rio and established himself as a friendly

Dutchman from Rotterdam who dealt in diamonds. This was not entirely an exaggeration, for Gottfried von Arnheim, as one of the commandants of an infamous women's concentration camp located in the forests of Silesia, had obtained by torture and death threats many freely volunteered gifts of costly jewelry from the terrified upper class women who, because their husbands or lovers or fathers had been suspect to the Third Reich as being either of the tainted Jewish blood or politically against Hitler, were in dire danger of losing their own lives. But this was not all that Gottfried von Arnheim took from these women, for he was an insatiable lecher whose rut was stimulated mainly by watching a pretty young girl or mature woman under the lash. In his post as commandant of a concentration camp, he had often amused himself by attending an interrogation of some attractive Czech or French or Polish girl in one of the windowless subterranean cells. In many instances, even from these condemned prisoners, he had been able to extricate valuable loot, since prisoners from the middle and upper classes of their own ethnic groups were specifically sent to his camp.

As he stood admiring the magnificent white sandy beach and the gently rolling blue waves of the vast ocean beyond him, he puffed at his Upmann and his beady cold gray eyes narrowed in reminiscence. He had never forgotten any of his charming, helpless, doomed prisoners. There had been a French girl by the name of Renee Chambrun, whose father had been suspected of being one of the leaders of the Maquis and whose mother had been a schoolteacher in Paris. Honore Chambrun had ultimately been captured and shot for guerrilla tactics against German soldiers, and a detail of men had been sent to his palatial home to appropriate all valuable objects d'art and any cash that could be found on the premises. He had been a banker before

Passion In Rio

the war, and he had diverted his own money into the Maquis in order to fight Hitler.

But they hadn't found Honore Chambrun's treasure, so the mother, Felice, a stately and beautiful woman of thirty-nine, and the daughter Renee were both sent to the same camp, and he had received orders to make them talk before they were put to death.

Their death was certain, because the Germans had no desire to release the wife and daughter of a known Resistance hero, who might themselves rally other French patriots to revolt. But Gottfried von Arnheim had not told either Felice or her daughter Renee that whether they talked or not, they would not leave alive. And he had profited in a most delicious way that even now he could remember, twenty-five years later.

First, he'd had Felice Chambrun brought into the interrogation room and stripped naked by two privates of the S.S. She had faced him with heroic composure, though her torturers had fondled and pinched her full round breasts and admired her pale white skin and mockingly loosened the prim oval bun of her dark brown hair and dragged it down below her shoulder blades. What a magnificent piece of kootzele she had been, Felice Chambrun! Then he had threatened her with torture, and she had spat in his face and refused to tell him where her husband's money was hidden. He had simply shrugged and ordered the soldiers to bring in Renee Chambrun.

Then, while the shrieking Felice was tied with her arms high above her head and standing on her toes, she had been forced to watch while the two soldiers had flung the slim black-haired teenager down on a low wide bench, strapped her wrists and ankles tightly and then torn off her dress and slip and left her in filmy bra and panties, gray lisle stockings with elastic garters at mid-thigh and dainty pumps. Gottfried von Arnheim had lit a cigar and seated himself on a footstool beside the bench on which Renee, terrified and weeping, struggled and squirmed. Carefully and deliberately he had puffed at the cigar until it glowed a fiery red, then flicked the hot ashes into the valley of her breasts, boldly pear-shaped love gourds which in her tumultuous breathing violently thrust against the thin bra, showing the rosy tips of her virgin nipples.

Felice Chambrun had weepingly implored him to show mercy on the innocent young girl, but he had ignored her. His back to her, he had touched the cigar's lighted end to Renee's ivory throat, then to her left armpit till the silky black private hair began to sizzle and Renee's piteous screams of "Maman, maman, sauve-moi, maman!" made his prick throb with savage ecstasy of anticipation.

Finally he had turned back to Felice Chambrun and in an arrogant guttural voice, informed her: "Frau Chambrun, you will either tell me where your husband concealed his money, which was used to finance criminal guerrilla attacks upon the soldiers of the Third Reich, or I will have my men take tweezers and pull out your daughter's pussy-hair. Then she will receive a whipping across her breasts from a good leather strap, and after that I shall let all my men fuck her as they please."

In despair, the handsome brown-haired matron had implored him to torture her, or ravish her, instead. But when she had seen Gottfried von Arnheim rip away the bra and apply the burning tip of his cigar to her daughter's left nipple, she capitulated. Hysterically sobbing, babbling incoherent words, and needing to be brought to composure with an occasional lash from a riding crop across her belly or inner thighs, Felice had at last told them where the treasure was. He had excused himself from the cell and telephoned the Gestapo leader in Paris, with orders to be called back at once as soon as the money was located. Then he and his men had gone to another cell to interrogate another unfortunate young woman. An hour later, after they had left her unconscious, her body covered, the call had come through from Paris that the money had been located.

So he had returned to the cell of the Chambrun bitch and her pretty pup, and set his two men on Felice Chambrun at once. One of the soldiers had fucked her, while the other buggered her from behind, thus sandwiching her buxom and voluptuous body. But she had been able to see that Gottfried von Arnheim had saved her daughter for himself. Ripping off Renee's panties, he had pinched and tickled her pussylips while the unhappy young brunette shrieked and sobbed and called upon her mother like an ingenuous child to save her. Gloatingly he had mounted the slim ivory-skinned teenager and taken her cherry. Then she had been turned over and strapped down again and he had taken the virginity of her asshole as well.

What a memorable session that had been! A week or two later, after he and his two men had tired of the two naked bitches, they had been dragged outside in the courtyard on a freezing late November morning, made to run a gauntlet of all the guards who belabored them with truncheons, crops and dogwhips, and then told to run for their lives. If they could reach the gate and touch it before the savage Belgian police dogs were set upon them, their lives would be spared, Gottfried von Arnheim had told them. He had watched, his eyes glittering with lust, his prick stiff in the fly of his military breeches, while the two stumbling naked women had made their way towards the gate three hundred yards away. Fifty yards before they reached it, he had blown a whistle, and four vicious dogs sprang after them, overtook then before they could touch the gate, and they had died under the slavering jaws of the beasts.

It had been a long time since he had so enjoyed himself, but now that the great Carnival was approaching, he meant to amuse himself in ways that he had almost forgotten since he had fled Germany and taken refuge in South America. He was now a respected and very wealthy *Carioca*, known as *Senhor* Hans Landau, a name which gave credence to his pretended Dutch ancestry. He was director of a novelty manufacturing firm, a firm whose major business at the moment was preparing souvenirs and costumes for the magnificent four-day pre-Lenten celebration. He owned an elegant house not far from the Maracana Stadium, in front of which was the Museum of the Indian, which housed a series of expositions on the different themes in the lives of Brazilian Indians. He had a handsome forty-year-old housekeeper who had come from Curaçao where it was rumored she had poisoned her husband because he had taken another woman. Also, he had a sultry, red-haired, twenty-five-year-old mistress, Marguerite Villefranche, whom he had discovered two years ago when she had been stranded after the financial failure of a Parisian Nightclub troupe that had been playing in one of Rio's swanky nightclubs.

The only trouble was that both these bitches would only fuck, and they wouldn't let themselves be manhandled the least bit. There was too much danger of a scandal if he were to take Marguerite or Amelia down to the cellar, tie them up to the beam, and whip them till they bled and then bugger them as he longed to do. But perhaps, now that the Carnival was nearly here, he might make some arrangements to abduct a pretty *Carioca* girl and, during the madness which would reign for four days and four nights, slake his pent up sadistic desires in one unforgettable orgy that would revive for him the

Passion In Rio

glorious past when he had been a vital power in Hitler's Third Reich.

He turned now to the bell captain, a cynical, mustachioed, tall rogue in his mid-thirties, and beckoned to him.

"The *Senhor* desires?"

"What's your name, fellow?"

"Heitor Bodegas, *Senhor* Landau, at you service. Is the suite satisfactory, *Senhor* Landau?"

"It is admirable, Heitor. Here's a little something for you." He handed the bell captain a sheaf of banknotes amounting to about fifty dollars in American money. Heitor Bodegas' crafty eyes widened with unexpected and delighted surprise, and he began effusively to express his thanks.

"I may have need of your services, Heitor. I daresay, as bell captain at the Copacabana Palace, you keep your eyes open and you know where certain pleasures may be obtained."

"I think I understand the *Senhor*."

"Not yet. But perhaps tomorrow evening you will take a glass of brandy with me, after your shift is over, naturally. We shall talk then. There will be many more of these gratuities if you succeed in helping me find what I'm looking for."

-6-

Lorna Destry looked carefully around the salon she had engaged at the Hotel Excelsior. It was quite elegantly furnished, and the view from the huge bay window out onto the white sandy beach and the glorious blue ocean was simply breathtaking. She had taken a suite simply because she had wanted to give herself a final treat, a kind of farewell indulgence. Because, after the Carnival, Lorna Destry was going to kill herself.

She wasn't even sure that she could pay for the suite during her stay. It was fifty dollars a day, and there would be meals and tips and doubtless a costume for the Carnival. And then of course some sightseeing, and a rental of a little cabana down at the beach so that she could change her clothes and go out there and swim if she wished. But right now, that didn't matter. She had about two hundred dollars left in American Express traveler's checks. With the two hundred dollars, she could bluff her way through this gala week of luxury, keeping enough for tips, the cabana and of course a new bathing suit. The meals she could charge. The Excelsior had a superb restaurant, and its 'Stadium' was very popular for late dinner and dancing, the intelligent-looking, slim and wiry English-speaking bellboy had told her. His name was Nuncialo, and he couldn't be more than eighteen or nineteen. As a matter of fact, what she didn't know—nor did the hotel management—was that Carlos was just seventeen, for he looked remarkably mature

Passion In Rio

for his age. And any woman who had ever taken him to bed by way of a kindly experiment had been most delightedly surprised. Carlos Nuncialo was what a *norteamericano* would call a real pussy-hound.

Lorna Destry was twenty-seven, tall—about five feet seven and a half inches in height, to be exact—with a somewhat angular face that made her look plain at first glance. Her auburn hair was coiffed in a fashionable upsweep with one large curl over the left ear, but it was lusterless. Though she had been living in Miami Beach for the past two years, her skin was an unhealthy pale white, and marred at the cheekbone and the base of her chin with a patch or two of acne. The highset shape of her cheekbones and the firm jawline made her look almost belligerent, and her mouth was perhaps a trifle too small and a bit too thin for sensuality. Her nose was small and straight with rather broadly flaring wings. Her shoulders might be said by a connoisseur to be just a trifle bony, without enough flesh on them. But if a man were to stop there and dismiss Lorna Destry, he would be making an unforgivable error. And several men had already done just that, which was one of the numerous reasons Lorna had for intending to terminate her life as soon as the great Carnival was over.

For even though she wore a tailored woolen dress that was really too bulky for her in this weather, nothing could hide the fact that she had a pair of widely spaced, full-blown, pear-shaped breasts and a slim waist that veered suddenly and dramatically as well as prick-stirringly into sumptuous haunches; broadly oval buttocks that undulated in the most salacious way whenever she walked. The narrow crease was sensuously placed and it seemed to widen at the base of those luscious bottomglobes. Her thighs also bore out the mellifluous promise of her hips and bottom, and her calves completed the ensemble, fine saucily contoured calves with agile muscles rippling in them at every step.

About an hour in a good beauty salon with a really conscientious counselor, a change of diet, a more interesting job than the one she'd had for the past two years, and a man could forget the plainness and sometimes even the gaunt loneliness of her face and fuck her to bubbling orgasm.

But because of the lack of such a man, Lorna Destry had mournfully decided there wasn't any more purpose in life and that she would go out in one final blaze of glory. One of her few friends had been working in a travel agency in the Bay of Biscayne Building and had given her a descriptive and illustrative brochure on Rio de Janeiro, concentrating on the annual pre-Lenten celebration. Lorna Destry had read the folder over and over in her lonely little room in old Mrs. Williams' boarding house on Summit Street, and then she had made her valorous decision. She had induced Betsy Terwiliger, her friend at the travel agency, to book her one of the best suites at the Hotel Excelsior for a week. Her credit was good enough to get her air fare down to Rio charged on a twelve-month basis, and she had told the Pan Am people that she'd leave her return date open because maybe she'd want to stay down there an extra couple of days. They hadn't questioned it. And so here she was now with one suitcase and about two hundred dollars left to her name and a bottle of sleeping pills she'd been accumulating pill by pill over the past year for just such a contingency as this.

"It's really very lovely," she said musingly as she stared down at the beach from the sixth floor.

"Yes, *Senhora*, it's one of the loveliest sights in the world," the handsome young bellboy enthusiastically rejoined. "Is there anything else that I can get for the *Senhora*?"

Passion In Rio

"No, I think not. Thank you very much. I'll just have a nap and then I'll go down to dinner."

"The *Senhora* has just come in by plane from the *Estados Unidos*, isn't that so?" Carlos Nuncialo courteously remarked. "In that case, it must have been a very tiring trip. I shall be very glad to bring the *Senhora* whatever she may desire. In the drawer of the writing desk there is a menu from the restaurant. You have only to call the operator and tell her that you wish Carlos."

"Why, that's very kind of you." Lorna Destry managed a faint smile. Now that she was here, now that she had seen Sugar Loaf Mountain and the dazzling bench and the row of swanky hotels, she felt more forsaken and lonely than ever before all her life. Because all this beauty had nothing to do with her, and there was no one here who knew who or what she was or even cared. And yet the graciousness of this seemed so unusual that it nearly made her cry, coming as it did when she was feeling thoroughly sorry for herself.

It wasn't that she didn't have reason. Lorna Destry had been told to her face at the age of fifteen by her drunken father that she was a homely bitch who had better get herself a decent job because she certainly was never going to hook a man with that pimply face of hers. She had for the most part outgrown the acne, but now and again, particularly when she was emotionally overwrought, a patch or two showed up just as now. This was caused by the excitement of the trip and also by the terrifying awareness of what she was planning.

She'd had two brothers older than herself, and of course her father and mother had made much of them. It hadn't mattered that one had landed in the reformatory for stealing a car at the age of seventeen and then gone on to bigger and better things, which had finally culminated in a Pittsburgh downtown alley one bleak November night, with her brother lying dead with a bullet in his brain from a night watchman's gun. He had been planning a big job, the theft of morphine from a medical supply warehouse.

Her parents had moved to Miami from their home in Pittsburgh when her father had come into a little money, thanks to her uncle's good luck on the stock market and his sympathy for his unlucky niece. But in Miami, her mother had got a job as a maid and she herself had really found very little except a job as a checker in a restaurant. She tabulated the price of the dishes on the waiter's tray, writing out the checks, and was used to being harassed by those who wanted a quick check for an impatient customer. She was called "Hey you!" by nearly all the help, including the boss. It paid just barely enough for her to have her own little room at the boarding house and to move away from her mother who was bitter after her father's death a year ago from a heart attack following a drunken brawl in a tavern. As for her other brother, he was somewhere on the West Coast, and sent back letters with an occasional five-dollar bill, boasting about his job. Her mother had believed it, but Lorna had found out that the 'job' was working in the tool shop of Folsom Prison where he had been sent for armed robbery.

Romance? Very little. In her senior year in high school, where she had been a brilliant student and believed that perhaps one day she might become a teacher, there had been one fellow who had taken her out to a movie and run his hand under her skirt and kissed her on the breast. She'd been so excited that she'd almost let him do everything to her in the back of the car parked in a dead end street late at night. Then she'd gone out on a few more dates with him, only to discover that he was doing it on a dare and that he was actually going to get money for winning the bet. She'd slapped his face and had a fit of hysterics in her own room until her father had taken the strap to her. And of course she hadn't been able, she hadn't dared, to tell him why she was carrying on like that.

She'd wanted to go to college, but of course there hadn't been any money and there'd only been a partial scholarship. She'd compromised by going to business school evenings and working during the day washing dishes in a cheap little Greek restaurant. There the boss, a fat man in his forties who pomaded his hair and thought himself to be a great lover, had pinched her bottom a couple of times and hinted that he'd like to give her a tumble in the back room. But he was married and had six children, and his wife came to the restaurant almost every day, a nagging, shrewish creature who, even if Lorna Destry had been interested in such a clandestine liaison, would have soon ferreted it out.

Yes, there'd been a few dates after that, hit or miss affairs, one or two blind dates arranged by her loyal friend Betsy. But somehow they'd never come back again, though they'd been very polite and very courteous the first time. And then, only last month, she'd felt that at last fate had given her a decent break. Two of the waiters had been taken sick that night, and the boss himself had come down with an attack of the flu. There was a very distinguished-looking man alone at a little table near the kitchen. He was busy looking around for water and butter, but the busboy had been ignoring him. Lorna Destry had taken it on herself to leave her stool just inside the kitchen to go out and serve him. He'd been so gracious, so kind, that she'd blushed at his praise. And then, after he'd had his meal and asked for his check, he'd beckoned to her, asked her name and whether he might call her some evening.

It had been just wonderful all that next week. His name had been Thomas Parkinson, he was forty-two, managed a franchised bottling company—one of the regional brands—and he wasn't married. He seemed genuinely interested in her, and after they'd had two dates, had invited her to his lovely little bungalow not far from the beach.

He'd given her French wine and played records for her, sitting with her on the couch with his arms around her shoulders. She'd been trembling, and she'd felt her pussy moisten and itch with longing. At last, she had told herself, someone was going to take an interest in her, someone who really cared, someone to whom she could give everything. She had so much to give, all the affection that had been dammed up all these years was waiting to be poured out on this gentle and considerate man. The age difference wasn't anything at all, not really. He was suntanned, beautifully dressed, he used the most elegant diction she'd ever heard, he had this beautifully furnished bungalow, and certainly a good deal of money. But best of all, he wanted her, she could tell that from the way he was pressing his thigh against hers, and tightening his arm around her.

And then everything had turned into a hideous nightmare. He'd whispered into her ear that he wanted to make love to her, and she'd almost swooned away and clung to him, putting her lips to his, feeling her nipples harden with longing. And then he'd taken her into the bedroom, and helped her undress until she was down to garter belt and panties and bra and hose and pumps.

Then, to her horrified dismay and revulsion, he'd stripped naked and, spreading his legs arrogantly, his hands on his hips, he'd growled, "All right, bitch, get down there and do me a blow job. You've got just the mouth for it." She'd protested. "But, Tom darling, I don't understand—don't you want to love me?"

And he'd answered: "Love you? That's a laugh, you long-legged tramp. You've got a face on you that would

Passion In Rio

stop a clock. But I want to give you a thrill, so get down there and suck me. If you're a good girl, I'll give you some dough. Maybe I'll even jack you off with my finger. Hell, bitch, I'm married, but my wife's out of town. She doesn't go in for Frenching."

She'd screamed at him, slapped him, pulled her dress on and rushed out of the bungalow, hailed the first passing cab and gone back to her lonely room and wept all night long.

And that was why now, just before the Carnival, Lorna Destry had decided to have one final fling, a never-to-be-forgotten taste of luxury that she could never afford in all her life, and then to die swiftly and painlessly, to finally achieve in oblivion the peace and the forgetfulness which she couldn't find in life.

- 7 -

To symbolize the beginning of the Carnival the next day, there was a gala display of fireworks from the side of Sugar Loaf Mountain, and those fortunate enough to be guests in the fine hotels along the beach, and whose rooms had spacious balconies, could sit outside in the balmy night air and enjoy the magnificent spectacle.

Miguel Valdes, the night porter at the Trocadero, was not privileged to watch this pyrotechnical preview of the pre-Lenten celebration. He had to work this evening, and he was grumbling to himself as Pedro Alicanzar, the baggageman from the airport, drove into the back courtyard with a heavy load of suitcases of guests who had either sent their baggage on ahead or had already arrived and were waiting for it.

"A good thing this load comes tonight, eh, Miguel old friend?" Pedro Alicanzar chuckled. He got down off the truck, rummaged in his overalls pocket and came out with a battered pipe and a badly worn tobacco pouch. "I'll help you this time, on account of it's the Carnival and nobody's going to work for the next couple of days. First let me have a smoke. A pipe is a good companion, Miguel. It's trustworthy, and once you've broken it in, it doesn't bite back, the way a woman will."

"You are right as always, Pedro," Miguel grumbled. He was thinking of Miranda, who at this very moment was probably trying on her Gypsy costume with the imitation gold earrings and that sparkling tiara, parading

Passion In Rio

before her mirror and doubtless making herself pretty for that son of a bitch, Francisco da Rucosta. He hadn't found out yet what Francisco was going to wear as a costume, but he knew one thing for sure: Miranda would be dancing with the bastard, and Miguel would have his jack knife. They'd be bound to be in the parade, and just one quick plunge of the knife and it would be all over for that fellow who fancied himself to be such a gift to women. In the hubbub of the Carnival, with all the firecrackers and the shouting, nobody would hear the scream of a man who got a knife thrust in the back. If he did it right, Miguel was sure, there might not even be a cry, not a sound. Francisco would just go down and be trampled by the marchers and nobody would think twice about it. Just some drunk who had celebrated a little too much in advance. And then he'd be rid of Francisco da Rucosta for good. And it would be Miranda's turn to learn a lesson. A good thrashing, locked up in her room until he came home and condescended to give her what she wanted between those squirmy long olive-skinned legs of her. That was the way to do it.

Pedro Alicanzar was a man of fifty, stooped from carrying heavy baggage these past thirty years, and he had a wife and four children, two of them already grown up and married. He was a good man, a little stupid, perhaps, but as least he knew his place and he pitched in and helped when he didn't have to, like tonight. And one thing was for certain, he never in the world had the problems that Miguel himself had with a gorgeous young wife like Miranda. It had been perhaps a mistake for Miguel to have wed a country girl and believe that he could satisfy her. The first year or so had been splendid, but now that she was a *Carioca*, now that she felt herself to be a citizen of Rio, she was looking around. She had plenty of experience in bed and she was a stunning piece, so it wasn't any wonder that others would try to grab her. Only what he didn't like was the sneaky way that this Francisco de Rucosta was going about it.

"That tastes good," Pedro sighed as he puffed at his pipe. "That's quite a display of fireworks tonight, you know.

"I've seen fireworks before," Miguel glumly replied. He took out a pack of cheap, strong cigarettes, lit one and uttered a long sigh. "In a way, I wish the Carnival were already over."

"That's no way to talk," Pedro rebuked him, clapping him on the back. "Don't tell me you have to work through it? Surely they can't be that hard-hearted. I'm finished as soon as I take this truck back to the airport. What about you?"

"Just tomorrow night, that's all. Then I get the next few nights off, and maybe I can have some fun," Miguel responded.

"It's a time to forget all your ties and cares, old friend," Pedro Alicanzar counseled. "You know, a vigorous rogue like you ought to be able to pick up some of those nice free and easy bitches you'll find in the street, girls who want to get screwed just because it's Carnival and they don't care by whom. I'll bet you can take care of them."

"No doubt about it. But they're not for me. You can pick up a good dose that way, when you don't know what you're putting your cock into. You, as an old married man, ought to know that best of all."

"Well, that's true enough, may the saints preserve us all for many more Carnivals to come," Pedro said cheerfully. "But seriously, hombre, don't you feel that you want to get your ashes hauled? I know you've got a gorgeous little wife and she's just about past the age for fucking anyhow. But it's funny that a man, no matter how old he is, never loses his desire, so long as he can get a stiff cock to do business with, *no es verdad?*"

Miguel nodded silently. There wasn't any point in torturing himself talking about pussy. Of course he meant to see what he could do when he had time off from the hotel, but the first order of business was getting rid of Francisco and then teaching Miranda her much-needed lesson. If there was any time left after that, he might just see what was to be offered. A man of his experience didn't rush headlong into an affair, even for just a night or an hour. There were too many things to be considered. "Let's get to work, then, so that you can have your holiday," he suggested. Pedro Alicanzar nodded in agreement, knocked out his pipe, stepped on the glowing coals, and walked over to the back of the truck to open it up so that he and Miguel could begin their chores.

Lawrence and Phyllis Valery had asked their mother's permission to go out in the street and watch all the preparations for the gala event which would begin tomorrow, and they also wanted to walk along the beach and see the fireworks. The brown-haired widow agreed. Her fortieth birthday was two days hence, at the very height of the Carnival. It was a landmark, and she still felt as desolate as she had when she had left New York thinking about her dead husband Daniel. She was sorry she had come. Of course, for the sake of the children, it was probably a good idea. They hadn't had a real vacation in some time, and they'd earned it. They were both high up on the scholastic list, Lawrence in his first year of college, and Phyllis to be graduated this June from high school. So they could afford a week or two away from school. But for her, it was almost torture to be here in a city where life and radiance and joy reigned, and yet to feel herself so alone with the gloomy thoughts of the tomb. She remembered the handsome headstone she had carved for her husband and the simple words she had had inscribed upon it: "Mourned by his loving wife, in deep remembrance of unforgettable companionship." The tombstone-cutter had tried to talk her into a simpler message, but she had insisted on it. She wanted all the world to know what she thought of poor Daniel. There would never be another man like him, businesslike and yet affectionate, considerate and practical, a man to whom you could talk and tell your problems without being laughed at or condescended to—he always took her seriously, respectfully and graciously.

She began to dab at her eyes and to feel sorry for herself. The beautiful apartment they had taken at the Hotel Metropole didn't mean a thing to her now. She walked out onto the balcony and stared at Sugar Loaf Mountain, saw the rockets and the Roman candles bursting their multicolored spray of dazzling light over the dark blue of the ocean far beyond and the now shadowy beach below, and she felt absolutely nothing.

Perhaps some food and a cool drink might help. She hadn't really cared about supper, and she'd let the children go downstairs to the restaurant and enjoy themselves. There wasn't any reason why she should deny them pleasure just because she wasn't in the mood for it herself. With a sigh, she walked over to the telephone and asked the operator to send up a bellboy with a room service menu.

By luck, the call went to Benito Lobirma, the soft-spoken youth who had brought in the luggage for Kay Arnold and Joanne Claremont. He was looking forward to the Carnival, the very first he would see in Rio, and he felt a swelling of native pride because now he wasn't from his little village anymore; he belonged to Rio because he worked at the Hotel Metropole and had a

Passion In Rio

little room in the boarding house about three miles away. There was an old widow who ran the boarding house, and she cooked wonderfully well, including many of the native dishes that he had come to enjoy back in his own little village.

But he was lonely, and he didn't have a girl yet, though many had made eyes at him here in the hotel. But the assistant manager, Senhor Arturo Pondarme, a very pompous and dignified man in his fifties, had given him a long lecture about the standards of service which the Hotel Metropole exacted from all its employees and how he must never, under any circumstances, become personally involved with any of the guests. He must serve them humbly and gracefully, calling no attention to himself, as if he were a well-trained robot without any personality or feelings whatsoever. Yet at the same time, to be sure, he must impress them with the diligence and the courtesy, so that they would have only praise during their stay and return next season.

He had done very well, and there had been no complaints against him. If he had been more attentive and been more aware of such things (for he was still unworldly), Benito Lobirma might have realized that many an attractive *norteamericana* cast eyes at him and had a secret desire to have him caress and kiss and fondle her to know what it would be like to have a South American lover. But Benito had been oblivious to the sly hints of some of the bored wealthy divorcees and the jet-set daughters of the rich who looked upon him for a moment and considered the possibility of amusing themselves for a short space in their quest for pleasure and new experiences.

Alice Valery went to the bathroom, took off her dress and stared at herself in her slip, bra and girdle, flesh-colored stockings and open-toe pumps. She was still attractive, surely. But she couldn't fool herself any longer by saying she was in her thirties, because two days from now would be her birthday and she couldn't lie to herself. No, at forty, her life was almost over and there wasn't much to look forward to. In a few years, Lawrence would be out of college and probably getting married. In about the same time, Phyllis, who was really a beauty, and who was already beginning to have boys flirt with her back in New York, would probably be married too. Then she'd really be alone. And it wasn't good for a woman to want to live with her children, once they were married. No, she didn't want to look forward to that, anyway. She had money enough so she could travel, but it was a lonely life at best. Shipboard acquaintances were ephemeral creatures, shallow and brittle, and they meant nothing and weren't remembered once the trip was over.

It was very warm, and she took off her slip, reached for her bathrobe and donned it just as the doorbell rang.

But in her haste, she didn't tie the belt tightly, and the first button was left open, which showed her plump round delightfully whiteskinned breasts hugged by the nylon bra, exposing the narrow valley of satiny soft flesh between them.

She opened the door and smiled at the young bellboy. "*Senhora, a su servicio,*" he said in his soft voice as he tendered her the room-service menu. "What may I bring the *Senhora*?"

"How very polite you are." Alice Valery smiled sadly at him as she took the menu and walked over towards the balcony. It was strange how warm she felt, for the air outside was actually cool. Benito Lobirma followed her respectfully, thinking that he had never seen as lovely a woman look so sad. Her dark brown eyes were tragically lusterless, and her mouth was curved dejectedly downwards instead of being turned up in a smile because tomorrow was Carnival. This was the *Senhora*

Passion In Rio

who had a grown son and daughter, he knew. They should be with their mother. It wasn't right to leave the mother alone, not before Carnival.

"You speak English, I notice," Alice Valery remarked as she studied the menu, then turned to the handsome black-haired youth.

"That is true *Senhora*. This is why I was given the job at the Hotel Metropole. And I speak a little Spanish, but mostly Portuguese, which is the national language of Rio. Is the Senhora feeling well?"

"Yes, thank you. Let me see now. Nothing too heavy. Perhaps some fruit, and a cold drink? Iced coffee, perhaps?"

"I will personally arrange it, *Senhora*. But the beef at the hotel is very good. You should try our *churrasco*, which is barbecued beef, pork and sausages in a very nice combination. Our chef is very good, *Senhora*."

"Perhaps tomorrow, because that's far too much for me to eat so late at night. Perhaps a sandwich, a little fruit and the iced coffee, that will do very nicely."

"I shall be back quickly, *Senhora*."

"Thank you. What's your name, young man?"

"Benito Lobirma, *a su servicio, Senhora*."

"Benito. What a pretty name, Benito." She tried to smile, because she thought that she had never seen so gentle and understanding a face. He couldn't be much more than seventeen or eighteen. And so mannerly, so well groomed, those soft limpid eyes and that light coffee colored skin, in a way like a young Rudolph Valentino. When she had been a girl, she had seen Valentino's movies, "The Sheik" and "Blood and Sand," and she had fallen madly in love with the black-haired, suave, romantic Italian actor. In some ways, this bellboy reminded her a little of her schoolgirl crush.

He had left the suite now, and Alice Valery walked slowly out onto the balcony to stare beyond the dark horizon towards the world she had left. It was dark, that world, dark because Daniel was gone and would never return to her. There was the water of the Atlantic, and beyond it was the city she called home for so long. There she was known, at least, and here she was an utter stranger. This young bellboy had been the first to show her any courtesy, any deference, and it somehow touched her.

If only she could put herself into the spirit of the Carnival and forget who and what she was. But after you had been with a man for many years, you adopted not only his mannerisms but his way of thinking. Daniel had never been promiscuous though certainly she would never have called him puritanical. He liked to look at a pretty girl, of course, but he had always been faithful to Alice. And there was a joy and a relish to their coming together at night, their bodies exulting in the vitality of youth and passion. Even after the honeymoon, even after the children, there had been secret delight in their cohesion. They knew each other so well, they could anticipate each other's moods, and a caress and a look would be enough to start Alice Valery's pussy to churning with a furious eagerness for love. Who was there now to bring this about, to tell her what her mirror tried to tell her, that her body was still desirable, that she still was capable of love and passion? No one.

Tears edged from the corners of her eyes, and she sighed wearily as she stared out at Sugar Loaf Mountain. The Carnival would be four glorious days and nights. Of course she would go along with Phyllis and Lawrence and try to forget. But on the dawn of the fifth day, when the Carnival was over, what then? Back to New York, back to her widow's weeds, back to taking pity and sympathy and condolences from friends who would gradually withdraw themselves from her. Once a woman was a widow, the people who were alive and

Passion In Rio

who used to be interested would gradually untangle themselves and pretend that she had never existed. Already her best friend, Deirdre Monahan, was beginning to make excuses as to why she couldn't come over to visit. That was the symptom that you were out of circulation...that you might as well be dead.

Once again there was a soft knock at the door and, almost startled by this restoration into the world of reality, Alice Valery stared back at the door. Then she remembered. Quickly she moved towards it and opened it. Benito Lobirma stood there with a tray, smiling gently at her. "May I serve the *Senhora*?" he asked in his soft, pleasant voice. "Perhaps out on the balcony. It is such a lovely night."

He set the tray down on the table, then went into a closet and brought out a table which he deftly set up outside on the balcony. Then, placing the tray atop it, he whisked off the covers to show Alice Valery what he had chosen for her: an appetizing sandwich of thick roast beef in dark bread, garnished with vegetables; a plate of assorted fruits, which included the wonderful *fruta de conde*, the custard apple of Brazil; *pitanga*, the Surinam cherry; and *jaboticaba*, a purplish fruit that grew directly on the tree trunk but was picked like a single grape; and finally a potato-like fruit called *sapota*.

"It looks delicious!" she exclaimed, smiling with pleased surprise. "Isn't that a cucumber they've put in the sandwich?"

"Yes, *Senhora*, it is called *maxixe*, it's eaten boiled. And there is the *baroa*, which you would call a carrot, which is cream-colored, as you see."

"It's new and very interesting, Benito."

"Thank you, *Senhora*. I took the liberty, instead of iced coffee, of having the chef prepare for you a *baba de moca*, which is made of sugar, eggs and coconut and tastes of honey."

"What a strange name. I would have thought that it meant mocha, which is a kind of coffee."

"Oh, no, *Senhora*," Benito smiled. "Translated, it means the saliva of a young girl. I ask your pardon if that offends you, *Senhora*."

"But why should it, Benito? I think this is very thoughtful of you. Here, let me pay you."

"You may sign the check if you wish, *Senhora* Valery."

"You know my name too!" Alice Valery delightedly exclaimed.

The young bellboy inclined his head respectfully. "Of course, *Senhora*. Since I am honored to serve you, I must know your name. I have asked the manager of the hotel to tell me who you are. I trust you are not distressed by my impudence?"

Alice Valery felt herself shiver with an inexplicable kind of anguished affection. It was as if suddenly here in this void, a strange city so far from home and one in which she felt herself utterly isolated, someone had come to her and caressed her and said, "Be of good faith, you are not forgotten, you are respected and loved." Tears welled in her eyes, and she had to bite her lips for self control as she went to her purse on the writing desk. "No, no, I want to pay this. And this is for you. Do I have the money right, Benito? I'm not too familiar with the rate of exchange here."

"The *Senhora* is more generous than she should be. You have given me twice the tip my services are worth, *Senhora* Valery. You must be careful, because even here in Rio, where all of us wish to make the *turistas* welcome, there are some, alas, who take unfair advantage because those from *norteamerica* can't always know our ways and our customs."

"That's quite all right, I want you to have it all,

Passion In Rio

Benito. Spend it and have fun at the Carnival. You will have a chance to take part in it, won't you?"

"Thank you, *Senhora* Valery, yes. Tomorrow I go off duty, and I will be back the evening the Carnival ends. But there is another very good boy at the Metropole and I will tell him to take good care of you and your children, *Senhora*. His name is Renaldo Vaneiros."

"That's very thoughtful of you. I will call the manager and tell him how pleased I am with you, Benito. In some ways, you're like my own son."

"It does not seem possible, *Senhora* Valery, because you are much too young."

Alice Valery could not help blushing, and, unbeknownst to her, the belt of her bathrobe fell undone, and the folds of the garment yawned to show her magnificently buxom body in the scanty dishabille of bra and girdle. Benito Labirma's eyes widened, and his mouth opened in a kind of sensual awe. He was still a virgin, but that was not to say he did not have demons of desire haunting him in the silence of the night in his little boarding-house room. Yet because he was chaste and pious, and because his parents had brought him up to be humble and self-effacing, he quickly averted his gaze. Alice Valery suddenly glanced at herself, gasped and then hastily belted and rebuttoned the bathrobe. For a moment she had shown herself to him in the way she used to tease her adored Daniel when they had both been very young. She had used to parade in the bedroom in just her scanties, as they then called them, in high-heeled pumps, hands on hips, pretending to be a call girl he had summoned, until he could stand no more and lunged for her and dragged her down atop him, and then they would giggle and squeal and twist and writhe and kiss and tongue until their flesh welded...the memory of this at once obliterated all the joy she had known from the young bellboy's thoughtful service. Once again tears shone in her eyes.

"Will not the *Senhora* eat?" he inquired anxiously.

"Oh yes, of course. I'm sorry. I guess my mind was far away, Benito."

"You are lonely then, for the *Estados Unidos*?"

"Yes, of course, but for much more than that. For my husband, Benito." Even as she spoke, Alice Valery was asking herself why she was baring her heart to an adolescent bellboy in a hotel in Rio de Janeiro. And yet there was such a sympathetic bond between them. His delicacy of manners in turning his face away when she had suddenly revealed too much of herself—why, not even in New York would a boy his age be so polite. Quite the contrary!

And suddenly a bold and daring plan leaped into her mind almost full born. "Benito—you said that you will be off the next few days, isn't that so?"

"Yes, *Senhora* Valery."

"I-I would pay you—it would mean a lot to me—my children will be going off by themselves, you understand. I would like very much to see some of this Carnival with someone who knows all about Rio. Do you think you could be my guide, Benito? I'd pay you very well."

"It wouldn't be necessary to pay me, *Senhora* Valery. It would be my pleasure. I shall be ready when you are."

"But how do I get in touch with you?"

"I am at a boarding house, *Senhora* Valery. It is on the *Calle de Tioarmina, Numero Seis*...I mean, Number Six. Perhaps tomorrow afternoon after lunch I could be of service to the *Senhora*?"

"Yes, oh yes! I-I'll call for you there about two o'clock. And—and thank you. Thank you, Benito."

"It is my pleasure and my honor, *Senhora* Valery. Till two, then, *Boa noite*." He smiled at her, inclined his head and went out of the suite. Alice Valery stood there

Passion In Rio

bemused, trembling, her eyes wide and luminous. She could feel her heart pounding rapidly. She felt as she had felt on the first forbidden date with Daniel—for her parents hadn't like him at all, had even forbidden her to see him. And she had gone to him under the pretext that she was going to visit a girlfriend, and her heart had been pounding just like this. Her hand went to her chest in order to try to stop her heart from beating so. It was to no avail, however, so she removed it. As she brought her hand down, it brushed over the triangle that contained her passion, sending a shiver up her spine. At once she remembered what it was like to be loved by a man. She passed her hand over her curly thatch of hair again, and again shivered. Was it necessary to have a man present to give her pleasure, she wondered. Now more daring, she sat on the couch and ran her finger along the crevice between her love lips. She was feeling uneasy about what she was doing, but she knew that there was no man to help her go about this necessary release. As her finger entered her love tunnel she thought of her Daniel, but found that too upsetting. She was too far gone in her physical manipulations to stop, so she closed her eyes and let her mind wander. She saw a summer night, a lovely candlelight restaurant, and a gracious waiter in a slim cut, tight fitting uniform. The creases in his trousers drove her eyes directly to his crotch, thickened with his cock. Atop his nipped waist sat a V-shaped torso around which a snug jacket without a shirt was clad. Alice's eyes roamed the hairy chest and developed pecs as she fingered the button within her. Her eyes lit on the waiter's nameplate just as her body shuddered with delight. "Benito," she exclaimed as her eyes widened with shock.

-8-

Lorna Destry was out on her balcony watching the fireworks from Sugar Loaf Mountain too and tears were running down her cheeks. It was like a fairyland. The balmy air, the marvelous sky with all the cumulus and the silver ball of the moon, the dark blue waters that seemed to form a pathway of glass on which one could walk forever and never reach the end of the world. She had on her bathrobe, bra and panties and slippers, but she couldn't sleep. There went a Roman candle, bursting away from the side of the mountain, with a dazzling shower of multi-colored lights. Each light was like a star, blazing swiftly, and then extinguished forever. She thought mournfully to herself, "I'm going to be like that, too. All those pills in the little bottle I packed in the bottom of my suitcase will make me soar like that star and then there'll be blackness and nothingness forever. Oh my God, I don't really want to die, but there's nothing else. I feel so cheap, so unwanted, so useless. And when my money's gone, when the Carnival's over, my life will be over too. But I've got to try to have some fun, some reason for coming here of all places. I could have just as easily gone to Jamaica or Hawaii, for that matter. I guess maybe I thought if I went to another country, I could pretend I was somebody important, by staying at this fancy hotel at prices I'll never be able to afford. I don't even have a return ticket back and when this two hundred dollars is gone, there's nothing."

Passion In Rio

Suddenly, she wanted a drink. Lorna Destry had never done much serious drinking. Oh, an occasional highball, and once or twice a glass of wine. And then the fellow who she had thought really loved her, that filthy beast who had wanted her to use her mouth on him and had contemptuously told her that that was all she was good for, he'd given her some white wine. What had he called it? Oh yes, she remembered...Chablis. Perhaps they had something like that here. She walked back to the writing desk on which the phone was placed, jiggled the hook and said. "Please send up a bellboy. I want to order something to drink."

"At once, *Senhora*," came the polite voice of the switch-board operator. Alicia Duarme was very proud of her English. She was thirty-five, chocolate-skinned, with magnificent breasts and ripe hips, and as soon as her shift was over at midnight, she was going up to the twelfth floor where in Room 1227 there was a man from Sydney, Australia. His name was Senhor James Linton, and she understood that he owned a big sheep ranch in the countryside beyond Sydney and that he also was a director of a bank there. He was fifty-two, had divorced his second wife six months ago, and came to Rio to enjoy himself, staying over for Carnival. He was extremely wealthy, she knew, for he had placed several calls to Sydney during the last week or two. One of them had been late at night, and he had come downstairs to tell her about it, and they had got to chatting, and he had put his hand on her arm and smiled at her and told her that he'd like to buy her a drink some evening when she was off duty.

Well, they'd had that drink, and tonight she was going to go to his room and let him fuck her. He had a tall wiry body and he didn't look his age at all, and he had the most piercing eyes, and the touch of his hand on her arm had told her right then and there that he was going to make her die of joy in bed. He liked her English too, and he had told her he was going to teach her some very naughty Australian songs tonight.

The call from Alicia Duarme was transferred to the hotel desk, where the night bell captain received it, and jerked his thumb at Carlos Nuncialto. "Take care of the *Senhora* in Numero 1026, Carlos," he said. "Don't forget, boy, you owe this job to me remember?"

"Si, amigo. That is very true. You know that I will share the tips with you."

The night bell captain, Porfirio Riacante, was fat and cynical and also engaged—without the hotel management's knowing it, to be sure—in the sale of narcotics to trusted customers. He chuckled and shook his head. "No so fast, Carlos. This *Senhora* Destry, the big boss doesn't think she's got too much *dineiro*. She's taken one of the most expensive suites we have, it costs fifty American dollars a day. And she has only one suitcase. That's not good. If she wants to order something expensive, don't let her sign for it. Be polite, but get the money. That's what *Senhor* Trougado, the big boss, told me to tell you."

"I understand, Porfirio."

The fat bell captain slapped the young Brazilian on the shoulder, gave him a broad wink: "Now I tell you what, Carlos, I know how much you like the *Senhora*s. Maybe she wants you in bed. She looks lonesome. And if she is that kind of *puta*, and we find out she doesn't have any *dineiro*, maybe you can break her in. There are lots of men with plenty of *cruzeiros* who will pay well to sleep with a *turista norteamericana*. So if she's broke, you get me, see if she'll fuck. Then we can make a deal with her, move her out of this fancy hotel to a little room I can rent not far from the Cafe Zum-Zum. That's where the rich *turistas* go to hear bossa nova when they're in Rio. Work on her, Carlos. And now

Passion In Rio

hurry up and see what the darling wants. If you play it right, you can make yourself her pretty *brinquedo!*"

"I'm not any woman's toy, Porfirio." Carlos drew himself up indignantly. "When a woman goes to be with me, she does it for myself and because I am handsome and young and can do it to her many times. But now I will hurry and see what the *Senhora* Destry wants, and I will remember all you have told me."

Lorna Destry admitted the young Brazilian bellboy who gave her his most courtly bow and presented her with a menu, on the back of which a beverage list was printed. "I am at the service of the lovely *Senhora*," he murmured.

Lorna Destry blushed. The title with which Carlos Nuncialto had addressed her was, she understood, appropriate to a married woman, but the adjective he had employed was absolutely new to her experience. No man had ever told her that she was lovely, and she was realistic enough to know that in many ways, at least facially, she had no appeal for the opposite sex. She stammered an inaudible thanks and turned over the menu, which was written in Portuguese with English translations for the turistas. "I think just a cold drink of any kind, and I'll leave it to you," she stammered.

"The *Senhora* is very kind to rely on my judgement," Carlos Nuncialto murmured. He was appraising Lorna in her bathrobe. It was true that the face of this *gringa* was certainly not the most attractive in the world, but her body was a different matter. Those *tetas* of hers were like pears, lush and firm, ready to have mouths all over them, and he could see the nipples thrusting against the thin material of the bathrobe. She had long legs, which delighted him. Her calves were long and well-toned, looking like they would feel just fine wrapped around his waist, if he were to give her what makes women happy. In the dark, it wouldn't matter that there were a few pimples on her face. But he remembered what Porfirio had told him. "It is late, *Senhora* Destry, and I may have some trouble getting what you wish from the bar. But perhaps if you would pay me, I could see to it that your needs are served," he intimated.

Lorna bit her lips. She wanted to hold onto that paltry two hundred dollars as long as she could because it was a kind of symbol; when all of those traveler's checks were gone, that would be the day on which she would empty the bottle of sleeping pills and drink them down with a glass of water and then wait for the peaceful and painless finale to her useless life.

She debated a moment with herself, and then moved over to the dresser, opened the top drawer and from under a neatly folded scarf, took out her purse, opened it, and took out a coin purse which contained the equivalent of five American dollars in change. As she hesitated, she wasn't aware that Carlos Nuncialto had taken a quick glance into the contents of her purse and seen only that one thin black book of American Express traveler's checks. No jewelry, nothing ostentatious, nothing that would indicate that the *Senhora* Destry had ample and unlimited funds. And in a suite which cost fifty American dollars a day, it was understandable that the management of this hotel felt happier when there was more security and collateral displayed. Thus far this *gringa* had called room service about four times and signed the check on each occasion, and according to Porfirio, her tips had amounted to less than two American dollars, or something like twenty-two hundred *cruzeiros*. This was not the way a wealthy *norteamericana* tipped.

Destiny is changed by many little things, seemingly inconsequential in themselves. Carlos Nuncialto, though only seventeen, was already an inveterate cocksmith.

Passion In Rio

He had begun his sexual education at the tender age of thirteen when the aunt of a next-door playmate had noticed his limpid eyes and slim young body and cold-bloodedly seduced him. It hadn't taken him long to take the upper hand over this buxom *Carioca* who was nearing her fortieth year and to get her to give him extravagant presents for the privilege of being fucked. His friend never seemed to realize that every time they played hide-and-seek Carlos would invariably end up in the closet of the aunt's bedroom. As soon as being tagged to be "it," Carlos would run to the boudoir and Nancita would bolt the door. With the energy of a teenager, he would strip in no time flat, stalking the lovely Nancita around her room, swinging his prick as he walked. If Nancita was scared of his huge dong, she never showed it, as she always greeted him wearing nothing but a silk robe and a pair of heels. She would already be wet from fingering herself, secure in the knowledge that her fuckmaster was in the house, ready to service her willing pussy.

"Carlos needs a new bicycle," he would snarl.

"What do you want for it," came the response, as Nancita ran her palms over her pointed breasts. They sat together high and firm on her chest, and she loved having Carlos suck on her nipples, and sometimes bite them.

"I want your dripping pussy on my tool. Now!"

With that, Nancita would throw off her robe and lay down on the bed awaiting Carlos' manstick to plunge into her. As soon as he stuck it in her hot hole and started pumping her, her legs were around him, her fingers clawing his back.

"Fuck me, boy. Fuck me for your new toy. Make me feel you up there. Give it to me good. I need you in me. Oh, yes. Fuck me."

One last long thrust and his seed would explode from

within him, and end up dripping out around Nancita's furry saddle. As she would shower, Carlos would unbolt the door, slipping into the closet to get dressed, and wait to be found by his friend.

But that was several years ago, and now he had been hired on Porfirio's recommendation, which carried a great deal of weight with the hotel management. Porfirio had seen the potential in this soft-spoken sleek youth, and had envisioned how some of the rich tourist women would be mad for Carlos. There would be profit in such yearning, and of course the grateful novice would be obliged to divide his extra-curricular earnings with the bell captain.

However, Carlos Nuncialto, about a month ago, had fallen in love—as much as his narcissistic ego permitted him to do so—with a beautiful young *Carioca* girl with green eyes and coffee-colored skin, part German and part Indian. Her name was Tianha Santos, she was eighteen, and the daughter of one of the subchefs at the Trocadero Hotel. Tianha was ravishingly beautiful, and he knew that she wasn't a virgin, but she played it that way. She was as much aware of her power over the male as he was of his over the female, so it was a kind of duel between them. She wouldn't yield unless he bought her a very expensive Carnival costume because she had a mad desire to go to the masked costume ball at the Hotel Copacabana Palace. Not only that, a ticket to that gala event would cost as much as a hundred American dollars, besides being very hard to get. She had told him two nights ago that he might take her flower if he would buy her the costume and a ticket for the masked ball. Well, this was Friday night, and tomorrow the Carnival began. Porfirio knew someone who could get him the ticket. And he had already saved enough to buy her a superb costume, that of a mermaid in silver cloth and gilt. But he lacked about seventy of the dollars neces-

Passion In Rio

sary for that ticket, and Porfirio wasn't going to hold it after ten o'clock tomorrow morning.

Accordingly, he made a bold decision. Intuitively, he knew that Lorna Destry was alone and in a blue mood, and he rightly guessed that she had come to Rio just for the Carnival to distract herself from what was probably a very mundane and cheerless existence back in the *Estados Unidos*.

"I should like, by way of welcoming the lovely *Senhora* to Rio," he practically murmured, "to treat her to a drink, if she will allow me."

Lorna Destry fumbled with the coin purse, looked up at the bellboy openmouthed. Then once again she blushed, and this time she actually looked pretty, like a young girl who has just been paid an incredible compliment. "Why—that—how very nice of you—what's your name?"

"Carlos, *Senhora*."

"I-I'm not really a—how do you say it, *Senhora*. I'm not married."

"But that is impossible."

"Oh? Why do you say that?" Lorna Destry was immediately intrigued by this unexpected retort.

"I do not wish the *Senhora* to be angry with me, I am only a servant here to see to her wishes. But if I were free, if I were a man who could say what he wished, I would have much to say to the lovely *Senhora*," Carlos Nuncialto slyly continued.

"I want you to say what you mean, C-Carlos. Please!"

"Very well then. I was going to say—and you will forgive me if I offend you—that the *Senhora* is so lovely and desirable that I cannot believe a man has not already made her his for life."

Lorna Destry gasped, her eyes very wide, while blushes spread to her throat and ears. Carlos Nuncialto was looking at her in the most adoring way, his hands clasped as if he were about to make a romantic declaration of love. She felt herself trembling. "The *Senhora* is not offended?" he anxiously demanded.

Lorna Destry shook her head, too moved to speak. "Thank you, *Senhora*. Then let me bring something that will be delightfully refreshing and I shall be back at once."

He bowed again, turned and was gone. Lorna Destry shut the door and leaned against it, closing her eyes and shuddering. A warm flux seemed to have invaded the flesh of her inner thighs and there was a tingling in her pussy. Her breasts began to rise and fall more quickly now, accentuating their fullness, and the nipples were aching with desire. Was in possible? Had she come here to die only to be saved by the unexpected love of a handsome boy like this? Oh God, if only it were true! If only she could have just one happy hour before she took those sleeping pills, something to remember, to carry with her into the timeless void of eternity!

Carlos Nuncialto was downstairs at the bar, digging into his trousers pocket for the necessary *cruzeiros* to pay Guido, the lantern-jawed Italian bartender who, rumor had it, had left Rome hurriedly to come to this job in Rio because he had got his girl into trouble and bought her an abortion which had killed her. He beckoned to the gloomy-looking Italian with an superior air. "Prepare for me, Guido," he said with an air of detached insolence, as if he were a paying guest in the hotel's most costly suite, "a double *cachaca* and mix it well with lemon juice and sugar. The *Senhora* Destry has never tried our famous *batida*."

"I see," Guido chuckled nastily with a lewd wink. "Doubtless you are going to spend the night with the *Senhora*. Perhaps you had better let me sell you some canabis, to make her passionate enough to last through the Carnival."

Passion In Rio

"That won't be necessary," Carlos Nuncialto austerely reproved the Italian bartender. "She pants for me already. She has not had a man in so long, if at all, that I will be like a strong young god between her legs. So make the *batida* strong, Guido. Here is the money for it. Can you get me something from the coffee shop?"

"It's late, and it will cost you extra if I talk to the cook. What do you want, boy?"

"Tonight I am a man, not a boy. Attention to that, Guido. Let me see. Since the *Senhora* is a newcomer to our beautiful city of *Cariocas*, I think she might enjoy a puree of mayo. Oh yes, and some *dolce do leite* will be a treat for her also."

"She must be scrawny, that one," Guido cynically commented as he began to blend the popular national drink, a colorless alcohol very much like the Peruvian pisco and the Mexican tequila, which is made of rum and is 98-proof. The *cachaca* itself cost about thirty American cents a shot, and therefore the double drink blended as Carlos had ordered it cost him about seventy-five American cents. Guido served this in an earthen pitcher, with two large glasses, and then, gesturing to his helper Isidro, an equally gloomy looking, very tall and thin Spaniard from Barcelona, to take over the bar, disappeared on his errand to the kitchen.

About five minutes later, he returned with the two desserts, which he set on the same tray, and then, folding his arms, demanded. "Let me have the *dineiro*, and my tip as well. A man must live."

"So he must if he has something to live for, Guido," Carlos gaily replied as he delved into his trousers pocket, took out his wallet and paid the bartender, adding the equivalent of a thirty-cent tip which Guido grumblingly accepted as being only about half his due.

Carlos glanced up at the clock on the wall and smiled to himself. In fifteen minutes, his shift would be over and he could very well spend the night with the *Senhora* Destry. He would try to break her in, and then he would talk to Porfirio. If he was lucky enough, he might get enough money from her to pay for Tianha's ticket to the masked ball at the Copacabana Palace. The little bitch was worth it. She had the most magnificent *tetas* he had ever seen in his life, and a behind that made him want to harpoon her right between those plump round insolent high-placed cheeks of hers. She had a skin like honey, sweet and moist, and its cafe-au-lait hue had made him dream lustfully the past few nights. In the darkness, this *gringa* he intended to plow would serve very well as a substitute. He would pretend that she was Tianha and he would really give it to her. She would expire with joy in his embrace, and she would be so grateful that she would give him all the money in her purse. He smiled wisely to himself, a sophisticate and embryonic extortionist already at his tender age.

"Here you are, *Senhora* Destry," Carlos Nuncialto purred as the Miami waitress opened the door to him. "I have here something very special, just for you, *Senhora*."

"Oh, it's too much! You ought not to have done it, you must let me pay you!"

Carlos carried the tray out to the table on the balcony. "The fireworks are still blazing," he announced, as if he himself had created the dazzling spectacle which lighted the distant sky. "You must assuredly be at your ease out here and enjoy what I have brought you."

Lorna Destry blushed again and followed him out onto the balcony. He drew out her chair carefully, seating her as if she were royalty, and his slim long artistic fingers brushed her shoulders as he drew back in an attitude of deference. "I have here something very special which we enjoy at times like these, *Senhora* Destry," he explained. "One is flavored with caramel, and the other is custard which has bits of orange mashed up in it. But you must try this drink, because it is our national drink and we are very proud of it. Let me pour it for you, *Senhora* Destry."

"C-Carlos, won't you join me?" Lorna Destry found herself asking with almost a plaintive tone to her voice.

Carlos glanced swiftly at his wristwatch. It had been the present of a fat old turistla a month ago, a woman who had a double chin and a wig who came from St. Louis and was very rich. She had thought herself so clever in making him seduce her, and she hadn't known in her fatuous delight at having him fuck her that he had deftly filched at least fifty American dollars out of her purse which lay open on the laundry hamper in the bathroom. She bought the watch for him and even had his initials engraved on it: "To C.N. from Edna D." It lacked two minutes before his shift was over. Well, Porfirio wouldn't mind at all, not if he was doing business already. And he was. "It would be a great honor for me, *Senhora* Destry."

"Please do call me Lorna. And I'll call you Carlos. You're so nice, so thoughtful. Are all the people in Rio like you?"

"They try to be, when they have the service of lovely ladies like you as their duty," the Brazilian youth flatteringly responded. He seated himself across from her, and stared at her as if rapt with enchantment. Again her face flamed. "Please pardon me, Lorna—you are sure that I may call you this and that it will not offend you?"

"Oh, I want you to, Carlos!"

"Then it is that I have never seen one so lovely, as the moonlight falls upon your face, Lorna. You are a queen of Carnival. But I am only a humble bellboy and I am a native from a little *favela*, and I should not dare speak this way to you, a rich norteamericana."

"Oh but you must—I mean," Lorna blurted, and suddenly took up her glass of *cachaca* and took a long sip. "Oh, it's delicious! I want you to say whatever you think, Carlos. After all, it's Carnival, isn't it? But you see, I'm not rich, not really. And—and I don't have very much money, and I really shouldn't be here at all."

"No, Lorna?"

"Oh no! I-I have a job very much like yours back in Miami, Carlos. I wait on customers in a restaurant."

Only a flicker of disappointment crossed his face. He had been prepared for this. But now it needed only the subtle blandishments of which he was capable to turn her into a woman desperate for love, one who would become a puppet at his will and whim. "But I'm very glad you told me this, Lorna." He leaned forward towards her, a dazzling smile on his soft, sensual lip. "Because now I can say to you what is in my heart. If you were a rich *turista*, I-I would have no chance at all. It is that I am very fond of you, Lorna. I have admired you every day since the first day you came to this hotel."

"Really? Oh Carlos, you make me so happy—you mustn't say it if you don't mean it, it would kill me!" Her voice choked with emotion, and she bit her lips and looked down at the table.

"I do not lie when I am in the presence of a beautiful woman such as you, Lorna," was his guileful answer. "That is why I could not believe when you told me you were not married. That no man would have the wisdom to see in you such a queen of beauty, with such a beautiful body and such lovely eyes and such a sweet mouth."

Lorna Destry was almost crying. Never in her life had she known such happiness. She seized the glass and almost drained it, wanting to distract herself, thinking that perhaps the elixir of that potently blended rum drink would perpetuate this moment for all eternity. His soft brown eyes lingered on her, his red moist lips

Passion In Rio

curved in a tender smile, and he was attentive and gentle. He would drive out all the memory of that beast who had wanted her to die.

"But you must eat the desserts I have brought you, Lorna."

"Oh please, Carlos, it's too much. Sit beside me and share them with me, please!" she murmured, her voice unsteady with the pent-up longing that all the years of wretched frustration and disappointment had brought her.

"Your wish is my command, *querida* Lorna." He took his chair and brought it beside her, and seated himself and very gently put his left arm around her waist. Then he drew back, and gasped, pretending vexation with himself. "But I go too far! Forgive me, Lorna—I was carried away. I ought not to have touched you. I am too humble, too unworthy."

"Oh Carlos, not you! You're so good, so kind, so sensitive! Please—I-I want you to do it—hold me, Carlos, I'm so lonely, you're the only person I know in all Rio and it's Carnival time!" She turned to him, her eyes glistening with tears, her face pleading and poignant.

"Then, out of my heart, I must do this," Carlos Nuncialto murmured. He put his hands on her shoulders, leaned forward and kissed her on the mouth.

Lorna Destry melted. She uttered a whimpering little sigh, nearly a sob, and clung to him desperately as if she were drowning and he were her only salvation. She gave him her mouth, her eyes closed, her breasts rising and falling violently in the turbulence of this strange new and deliriously thrilling emotion. He wanted her, he desired her for herself, oh blessed impulse that had brought her to Rio to be wakened into life and not to die! For now she didn't want to die, she didn't want those sleeping pills at all. It didn't matter that the money would soon be gone and that she didn't even have a ticket back to Miami. Nothing mattered except tonight, the eve of the Carnival, with Carlos beside her and the warm night and the fireworks and the drink he had made her take, which was already beginning to make her warm and glowing and alive for the first time.

Thus encouraged, Carlos Nuncialto glided his slim long fingers from her shoulders down to her swelling breasts, and Lorna Destry felt his hands cup her bosom with a masterful possessiveness while his warm moist mouth merged over hers, silencing the slightest protest. Yet she had none to make. Forgetting himself for a minute, Carlos let his fingers find her nipple and tweak it. Her heart beat faster, and a warm flood of desire churned between her long thighs, which had begun to twitch and flex with muscular contractions that betrayed her physical tumescence. For Lorna Destry was now ready to be fucked, her body clamored for it, and with all her heart and soul she desired nothing more than to expire in this handsome Brazilian youth's arms, yielding herself to him fully and gratefully in the joy of Carnival.

"*Te quiero*, Lorna," he whispered, when at last he ended the kiss, his fingers stroking her panting bosom, as she swayed against him, her arms locked about his neck, her face crimson, but not with embarrassment now, only with an overweening rapture. "Do you understand what I am saying, sweet little bird? Do not fly from me, your Carlos. *Te quiero mucho*!"

"Oh yes, yes, I do...oh Carlos, yes, I want you so much, so very much...I love you!" Lorna panted.

"Come on, come to bed, my beautiful one, my queen of the Carnival," his voice was low and husky with simulated passion. He rose, his fingertips plucking at her nipples till they ached with longing. Lorna Destry moaned and stumbled to her feet, leaning against him, her head against his chest. His hands glided down her hips, found her buttocks and began to knead them through the

Passion In Rio

bathrobe. And she could feel his swollen prick thrusting vehemently against the fly of his trousers.

"Ohhh, oh Carlos!" she moaned as she felt his fingers waken hitherto unknown sensations in her quivering body.

He stooped and lifted her up in his arms and bore her off to the ornately furnished bedroom which the management provided for those who could pay the tab of fifty dollars a day. He loosened the belt of her bathrobe and unbuttoned the buttons and spread it out on either side of her, as a cocoon is split asunder. And then very swiftly he began to undress, while Lorna turned her face to one side and shivered, closing her eyes and surrendering herself. Her bosom rose frantically against the thin bra, and her loins ached and were heavy with lust beneath the clinging panties. She could not help rubbing her thighs together, in her agitation. She was half afraid, and yet even more afraid that at the last moment this beautiful dream would end and she would find herself alone on this bed on this night before the Carnival.

But now Carlos Nuncialto was naked, his coffee-colored skin glossy and sleek with the health of youth. His penis was superbly virile, that of a full grown man. It was no wonder that the fat old *Senhora* Edna had been crazy about him. He had had to close his eyes and pretend to be overcome by her beauty when he had got between her thighs, but surprisingly enough, her cunt had been quite tight and rather hot. The poor bitch probably hadn't had a good reaming in a generation, and so he had obliged her. Even so, she'd got off much too lightly for all he'd given her for the paltry money and that wristwatch she'd bought him. The next time he would know better. Right now he knew better, and he knew what he would going to do with Lorna Destry. He was going to turn her into a whore who would fill his pockets so that he could enjoy Tianha whenever he wished.

Lorna Destry whimpered as his skillful fingers gently unhooked the bra and drew it from her, and she hardly heard the words, in Portuguese, by which he expressed his feigned passion for her. Yet he was somewhat surprised at the beauty of her body. It belied her angular face and that touch of acne and the small thin mouth and the bony shoulders. Her *tetas* were like hard firm pears and the big rosy nipples were darkened now and stiff, they throbbed and vibrated with every breath. And her cunt was plump and thickly covered with dark auburn curls. She had long thighs, and the pale white skin of them made his cock ache with longing. It was going to be fine. He would pretend it was Tianha. His hands came down on her breasts now, dominating them again, squeezing and fondling them, as he lowered himself over her. His cocktip brushed the fronds of her snatch, and Lorna groaned and spread her legs still wider. "Oh Carlos, take me, take me, love me!"

He thrust himself forward against the lips of her vulva. Lorna Destry winced, for she was still virginal, but only in the flesh; already her mind yearned to be the woman he needed, to gratify him and to pleasure him as he had already pleasured her and enraptured her with his attentions.

She uttered a gasp when she felt his cockhead move forward inside her narrow channel, and she set her teeth to keep from crying out, lest she dissuade him from the accomplishment of what she longer for. Then with a gasp, she felt her body seared with a fiery sword, and she felt herself pierced and plundered, and even as she cried out, his mouth came down on hers, hard and relentless, his hands, slipped under her buttocks, his fingertips digging into the gradually widening crease between those nether hillocks, and he began to fuck

Passion In Rio

Lorna Destry with consummate vigor and the furious insistence of his young animal body.

She moaned and struggled with him, glorying in the pain, forgetting all her disappointments, even that hideous insult which the brute had directed against her when she had refused to put her mouth to his organ. She had become a woman at last. She was being fucked! She repeated the word in her mind a dozen times and more, deriving the most exquisite and salacious pleasure out of it each time. And then she flung her legs and arms around him, and intuitively she met his every charge with her own grinding force, struggling under him to achieve the ultimate of life which would negate the hopelessness of the death she had planned for herself.

She loved it. She couldn't get enough of Carlos' cock inside her. He was getting to be too much for her to bear. "Fuck me, Carlos. I need it badly. Show me what it's all about. Love me with your prick."

She was transfigured. Her face was no longer ugly or pimply, but luminous and relaxed and warm, the face of a woman in love, and her superb body strove with his younger, sinewy maleness to achieve an indescribable cohesion.

She felt him spurt inside her, and the dam of her own reservoir burst and her own love-juices merged with his. She lay fainting on the bed, whimpering with joy, feeling the heavens crash around her as the warm night air came in from the balcony and laved their naked bodies on the bed.

Two hours later, radiantly joyous in her nakedness, shameless, Lorna Destry stroked Carlos's head as he turned to her and pillowed himself on her breast. "My little love, my darling," she crooned, finding new words to express her inchoate feelings in this hour of transfiguration. She wasn't a humble waitress from Miami anymore, but a woman who is desired by a strong handsome South American lover. Life had begun all over again for her, and this time it was going to be glorious. "Oh Carlos, I want you to love me, I want to stay with you all the time."

"And I want you to be with me always, *querida* Lorna," Carlos Nuncialto whispered into her ear. Then he bent his head and took one of her nipples between his lips and began to suck at it, licking it with his tongue. His prick was hard again, because this bitch wasn't bad at all. All you had to do was avoid looking at her face, but her *tetas* and her behind were really marvelous. How she could twist and squirm when she felt herself getting it! It was a lot better than that *Senhora* Edna and what was best of all was that this bitch who thought he loved her was going to make him all the money he had ever wanted to have so that he could have a real sweetheart, that delicious and taunting and bitchy Tianha. "If only—but no, I mustn't say such things to you, dear Lorna."

"What mustn't you say—oh Carlos, not again? Oh my goodness, I certainly can't—you're wicked," Lorna Destry giggled as she felt his stiff cock pressing against her twitching, cream-stickied lovelips once again. "I want you all the time, every moment, dear Lorna," he breathed. His hands had again slipped under her behind and were digging into the resilient flesh, as he rode over her, planting his prick deeply into her, and then immobilizing himself. He was going to make her beg for it this time. He felt the contractions of her cuntwalls against his rooting ramrod, and he smiled to himself.

"Oh please, tell me what's on your mind, Carlos! Don't keep anything from me, please, darling!" Lorna begged.

Her arms were around him, she had wound her thighs over his, and she was arching herself, trying to

Passion In Rio

make him start that divine, that indescribably thrilling back-and-forth movement which scraped the crannies of her cunt and made her glory in being a woman again.

"Alas, darling Lorna, I want so much to go to the masked ball at the Copacabana Palace tomorrow. But it takes money I don't have."

"I'll give it to you, Carlos! If only you'll spend the time with me till the Carnival's over," Lorna Destry panted. She twisted and squirmed herself impatient now to have him fuck her again. Her mouth sought his, and her eyes stared deeply into his. "Oh darling, just love me again, for it's so thrilling!"

"I don't think I can get you into that ball, but I've always wanted to see it. But I'll tell you all about it. And tomorrow night, when it's over, I'll come back here and we'll do this again, no es verdad?" he whispered.

"Oh yes! Oh darling, take whatever you need. Money doesn't matter to me anymore. Just love me."

He smiled triumphantly. He drew his prick back slowly to the brink of her pussy, smiling again to himself as he heard her gasp, felt her arms and legs convulsively clutch him all the more tightly. He was going to get every penny she had in that little black book of traveler's checks, and then when she didn't have anything left, when the management demanded payment of the bill, he'd show her a way to settle the account and to stay with him for as long as she could take it. She wasn't going to have to know about Tianha until much later. It was so easy, it was like taking candy away from a baby.

But for now, he could afford to be generous. She really wasn't half bad, this *gringa*. She deserved a little something for what she was going to bring him. Murmuring soft Portuguese love-words into her panting throat, Carlos Nuncialto began to fuck Lorna Destry with a slow and vigorous regularity that soon brought her to the pitch of climactic rapture.

-9-

It was Saturday morning and the state of the city of Rio de Janeiro was one of collective dementia. Everything in the city was tightly shut, from shops to government offices. It was a circus for the masses put on by the masses themselves, a ritualistic celebration which sought to express their own most unattainable and magical desires. Already parades had started down the streets, but on Sunday night there would come the gala parade of the *samba escola*s down a broad avenue cleared of all traffic and before thousands of excited spectators who crowded into temporary open grandstands.

Gottfried von Arnheim, registered at the Copacabana Palace as Hans Landau, was in his bathrobe and slippers lounging out on the balcony, and the mustachioed, tall bell captain, Heitor Bodegas, was serving him breakfast. The bell captain wasn't concerned about the tip for this menial service which any of his minions could have handled; he had something of great personal interest for the *Senhor* Landau, which he would not entrust to anyone else. Early this morning he had had a phone call from fat old Porfirio who had excitedly told him that one of his young boys had found a real *gringa puta* who needed money very badly.

Lorna Destry had spent the most magical night of her life, but at dawn, when she wakened to find Carlos Nuncialto beside her, she was stricken with contrition

Passion In Rio

and guilt. In the cold light of dawn, the misery she had left behind her in Miami returned to plague her. After the Carnival was over, would this handsome young màn still be true to her, still desire her? And even if he did, how could she remain in Rio? Would she find a job or money or even a passport that would let her stay beyond the tourist visa? These were problems that had to be answered soon, for by midnight of next Wednesday, the great Carnival would come to an end and then there would be disillusionment for her again.

And yet, even as she studied his handsome face, relaxed in sleep and the healthy exhaustion of a young man who has shot his load four times between a woman's straining thighs—for Carlos had really outdone himself last night!—Lorna Destry felt a wave of tenderness rise in her. Gently she touched his face, kissed his nose and forehead, and, naked and shivering, closed her eyes to recall the magical moments of this seemingly never-ending night. Today the Carnival had begun. And Carlos had told her that there was a way the two of them could be together. He was mad about her. He had always wanted to make love to a *norteamericana*, and he would work hard for her and see that she could be with him. But she would have to help, too. This evening he would go to the masked ball, thanks to her generosity. He understood that she didn't have much money. On the other hand, there were ways of making a great deal. And during their last fuck, while her body had shuddered and strained towards the delirious orgasm, which his seemingly insatiable lovemaking was bringing about, he had slyly proposed what he had in mind.

While she had dozed about one in the morning, after their second fucking bout, Carlos Nuncialto had tiptoed into the hallway and telephoned Porfirio. And Porfirio had just had an exciting proposition from the bell captain at the Copacabana Palace. There was a very rich man there, who lived in Rio but was spending the Carnival at that luxurious hotel. He wanted a woman that he would whip and pretend that she was his humble slave-girl. He was prepared to pay many thousands of curzeiros, and there would be a big cut for Carlos if he could talk to *Senhora* Destry into it. The estimable Senhor Landau would gladly pay her hotel bill and even see to it that she had a ticket back home to whatever part of the *Estados Unidos* she desired to fly back to. Just for a few hours, that was all. And so Carlos had told Porfirio that he was going to arrange it.

Carlos Nuncialto opened his eyes and saw Lorna Destry peering anxiously at him. Her pear-shaped breasts dangled temptingly only a few inches away from his face, and he reached up with a yawn and cupped them in his hands, as he said *"Bon dia*, my Lorna."

"Oh Carlos, Carlos," Lorna Destry exclaimed in a choking voice. She moved towards him, mounting over him, putting her hands under his shoulders and passionately kissing him on the mouth, while his hands caressed her back and ass, pressing her tightly against him so that her furry crotch could rub against his momentarily dwindled prick. The light of morning was cruel to her. There were lines in her face, and the blotches of acne seemed to be inflamed from all her amorous activity. Just the same, she still had a terrific body. Her *tetas* were as firm and satiny as any he'd ever felt. Of course they wouldn't be nice as Tianha's, but that would come later. Perhaps late tonight after the ball, Tianha would have her costume too, the silver cloth costume of a mermaid, slashed along one side to show off her beautiful long thigh, and with a fishtail trailing along the floor, and with the imitation fins sewn along her back.

"It was so good last night, darling," Lorna Destry passionately murmured. "Oh Carlos, when I woke up and you were there asleep, I was so afraid for a

Passion In Rio

moment. It was as if you had died and gone away from me. And I'm all alone here, and you're the only one I know."

"You mustn't fret yourself, *querida*. Now listen, because there is something I must ask you. And if you will do it, it will prove that you love me, and then the two of us can be together for a long time. I have friend at the Ministry who will see that your visa will be extended so you can stay as long as you wish. And I'll find you a job, I swear I will."

"Oh Carlos, do you really mean it? Do you still want me?"

By now, the handsome Brazilian youth's cock had begun to throb and to stiffen, and his fingers squeezed Lorna Destry's bottomcheeks lasciviously as he forced her to squirm and to wriggle even more lubriciously over him. "What must I do, Carlos? I'll do anything you want, if only you'll stay with me," he heard her say, and he smiled with triumph.

"Then listen, dear Lorna. There is a very rich man who is a photographer," he lied, "he wishes to have a *norteamericana* pose for him, and he will tie her up and make her wear a costume such as prisoners wore many hundreds of years ago. And for this he will pay a great deal of money, and it will be ours, my beautiful dove, my lovely Lorna, so that we can have a little room together and be sweethearts. Would you like that?"

"Oh yes."

"I ask you to do only this for me, and it will only be for a few hours, and then we will both be rich," Carlos lied. His fingers continued to squeeze and caress Lorna's shivering bare bottomglobes. By now his stiff cockhead was prodding her moist and twitching pussylips, and at this moment Lorna Destry forgot all her self-recriminations and misgivings, for her body yearned desperately for a repeated cohesion that would reassure her that she was loved and desired by this handsome young Adonis.

"I'll do it, oh yes, Carlos! You tell this man I'll do it. Will you be there, to make sure everything's all right?"

"But of course, my darling one," again he lied.

And that was why, this, the first morning of the great Carnival, Heitor Bodegas was talking earnestly with the former commandant of a Nazi prison camp, a wanted war criminal who had hidden himself in Rio all these years.

Gottfried von Arnheim listened greedily to the details the cynical bell captain provided, for Porfirio had rhapsodically described the charms of Lorna Destry. The Nazi was thinking to himself that he would bring this woman to his house, take her down to the cellar, and then he would have his mistress, Marguerite Villefranche, come over to visit him and tell her jokingly that he had found another redhead. She would be furious. So furious, in fact, that she would gladly collaborate with him in helping him flog and torture this American bitch who was willing to sell herself for money. And once Marguerite had learned the joys of sadism, it would be even easier for him to enslave her as he had always longed to do. And after that, his handsome housekeeper from Curaçao, Amelia.

"Very well, Heitor," he said, his voice thickening with lustful anticipation. "I'm going to give you some money. You'll take it over to this fellow—what's his name, Porfirio?—you'll take it over to him, and you'll have him bring the woman to my house this evening about nine o'clock. Make sure nothing goes wrong. I trust you have brains enough not to tell your friend at the other hotel what I really want to do with her. And you don't think there's any danger?"

Heitor Bodegas shook his head. "Not in the least, *Senhor* Landau. I have learned that this woman has very

Passion In Rio

little money, she has no plane ticket back to the *Estados Unidos* and she is desperately in love with a young fool of a bellboy at her hotel. He's told her that if she does this with you, they'll both be rich enough to live together in paradise."

"Very well done! You shall have a bonus for that, naturlich. Here, I'll give you some money in advance now so you can make your deal with this Porfirio. And I count on you yourself, Heitor, to bring this bitch to me tonight."

-10-

Alice Valery found it difficult to engage a cab on Saturday afternoon, because the Carnival was in full sway and the streets were packed with celebrating *Cariocas*, many of them already wearing the gala costumes they would show off in the parade of the *escolas* on Sunday. But at last the doorman of the hotel managed to get her a limousine whose driver agreed, for triple the usual fee, to take her to the boarding-house where Benito Lobirma lived.

She could see that there were buntings and banners in gay colors, posters and placards, shop windows full of marvelous and imaginative decor in Carnival theme. One could already hear the shouting and the cheering and the singing with which the people of Rio greeted this pre-Lenten celebration, seeking in it a release from all their problems and tragedies, seeking in it a freedom of absolutely uninhibited and hedonistic pleasure. There would be time enough during Lent to be sober and to be grave about the future, to worry about poverty and the uncertainties of holding jobs that would pay enough to live. For the people in the impoverished *favelas*, these problems were uppermost—but not during these four days and nights of riotous enjoyment. They did not care whether they bargained their souls to the Devil for the rest of the year so long as they might have serene and unclouded joy during the Carnival!

Meanwhile, Alice's son and niece, Lawrence and

Passion In Rio

Phyllis, found themselves back in the suite about noon, having gone down to the beach to swim after breakfast, and Phyllis discovered a note.

"Larry, it's from your Mom. She's gone out and isn't sure when she'll be back. She wants us to have dinner in the hotel restaurant and do whatever we like this evening. Can you beat that?"

Both Lawrence and Phyllis were in their bathrobes, and still had on their swimsuits, which they had dried off in the little cabana on the beach. Phyllis's light brown hair was soaked from the water, and it was matted against her head, but still showed the helmet-type coiffure. Lawrence Valery stared eagerly at her, for the bathrobe shaped out her luscious figure, which he had seen through a hole in the wall back in the States. For a long time he'd wanted to fuck her, and now, he told himself, was the perfect opportunity. Just before they'd left New York, he'd gone to his favorite spying place and taken out the little plug of putty he always left covering his spy hole when he wasn't watching so that nobody could suspect what he was doing. And he'd seen his cousin lying in bed wearing just her bra, garter belt, and flesh-colored nylons, playing with herself. She'd had her finger stuck well up her pussy, and was moving it around slowly, crooning something to herself as she arched and twisted and squirmed. She was pretending that a man was fucking her, he was certain. And now, finding himself alone with her for the rest of the day, the long-pent-up desire to have her burst upon him with all the power of a love potion.

"Phyl, honey, that's great!" he said as he moved closer to her. "You know, I'm sure glad Mom came down here to Rio after my Dad died. She's been moping around so much it's pathetic. She needs to get away from all that. And it was nice of her to take us along."

"Uh-huh, it sure was," Phyllis agreed. She had a

saucy face, with very thick eyelashes over somewhat almond-shaped gray-green eyes, an uptilted supercilious little nose with very thin and widely flaring wings, and a pouting, ripe mouth, the lower lip of which was much fuller than its sweet red twin. Her skin had a milky pallor, extremely soft and satiny, and Lawrence Valery knew secretly that between her delightfully rounded, rather plump thighs there was a thick forest of dark brown hair over her cunt. The mere thought of this made his prick itch and throb, especially in his tight nylon swim trunks, and he ground his teeth with maddening frustration. She had gorgeous bubbies too, for he'd seen them many times. They were saucy, uptilting, somewhat pendant, but very trim and widely spaced on her milky chest. They had very light coral circles, quite wide, with dainty, rosy tips. They were darker and stiffer, he knew, when she played with herself. Her hands were soft and small, her fingers very delicately tapering. The thought of them on his cock, tickling his balls, grasping his shaft, guiding it to her love-center, made him close his eyes and sway with the mad fever of lust.

And now that he stood next to her, he could smell the freshness of her skin mingled with the pleasant humidity of her body, which her wet suit gave her. Her feet were bare and thrust into sandals and there were grains of sand on her dainty little toes. He could see her bare ankles, slim and delightfully chiseled, and the lovely graceful rounded curves of her naked calves. He felt his prick throb with a furious energy.

"Want some lunch, Larry?" Phyllis asked. She unbelted her bathrobe, tossed it over the back of the armchair and turned to go towards the bathroom. Her sturdy, tall cousin uttered a stifled gasp of desire. His eyes fixed on the jouncy, closely spaced, upstandingly rounded cheeks of her behind, watching them undulate

Passion In Rio

and shift as she walked. And then he cast aside all restraint and moral scruple, for the incestuous fury that filled his virile young body could no longer be denied, whetted as it was by his remembrance of her naked body when he had spied on her.

He caught her by the shoulders. "Don't go, Phyl baby. Please don't go yet. You're so gorgeous—you're stacked," he panted. He twisted her around and then his hands grabbed for her bottom and pulled her tightly against him, mashing his hard rooting prick against her crotch.

"Larry—what are you—no, Larry—please don't you're crazy Larry, I said stop it," Phyllis cried, her eyes dilating with alarm as she saw the narrowed, glittering stare of her cousin on her lovely, flushed face.

"I've got to have you, Phyl. You don't know how much I've wanted to. Back home, I've watched you take off all your clothes, get naked, and you don't know what it did to me," he blurted.

"You're out of your mind—I'm your cousin, Larry—please—stop it, don't—I'll tell your Mom if you don't let me go!"

"No you won't," he panted hoarsely. "You know why you won't tell her? Because then I'll tell her that I saw you playing with yourself, baby! Sure I did!"

"You're absolutely crazy—what are you saying? You never saw me."

"Oh, yes I did, Phyl!"

His fingers were kneading her buttocks now, forcing her against him, and exultantly he felt his prick prod against the soft plump mount of her cunt, hidden from him by only the thin stuff of the bathing suit.

"There's a little hole in the wall between your room and mine, Phyl. I saw plenty, don't think I didn't. I can even tell you what you wore that time you were playing with yourself, right after Dan Perry gave you a lift home from school. You had on a black garter belt—and boy, if Mom ever found out you've got such slinky undies, she'd take a hairbrush to your bare ass, she sure would! A black garter belt, real sheer stockings, and that's all. You didn't even have a bra on. I could see your titties plain as day, like little puppies with pink noses. And you put your finger right on that hairy slit of yours and started diddling yourself! You were all hot, and were pretending that Dan was there in bed with you, weren't you, Phyl?"

"Stop it—no, I won't listen to such talk—it's dirty—I never did such a thing—Larry, please, you're hurting me, let go of me!" Phyllis Valery wailed. She tried to struggle, but he had grabbed both her wrists with his left hand and pinned them behind her back, while his right leg clenched around both of hers to prevent her kicking. He was grinding himself forcibly against her snatch, and now his face, flushed and contorted, loomed over hers, for he was a good four inches taller than she was. Her eyes were hugely dilated, humid and incredulous at this avowal of the unholy rut her own cousin had for her body. His other hand was fondling her bottom, and now it moved up to one of her breasts. Then suddenly he inserted it inside the bathing suit and cupped one of those lovely warm satiny globes, his thumbpad rubbing her nipple. Desperate, Phyllis tried to break away, to jerk his wrists free, but she couldn't.

"You've got a tiny little birthmark on your right leg, right near your pussy, too," he went on in a hoarse, trembling voice. "You've got the sweetest ass I ever saw, such nice white skin. You know you want it, Phyl. You know you've got hot pants for Dan, and he's not here. But I am. I won't get you in trouble, I've got safes."

"You—you're absolutely insane—how can you think of such a horrible thing with your own cousin?"

"Don't give me that song and dance, Phyl!" he

sneered. "I'm better than Dan. You watch and see if I'm not. Come on, let's go into the bedroom and have some fun."

"Please—no, no I don't want to!" she wailed.

With a muttered curse, Lawrence Valery released her, only to seize her in his arms, lift her up in the air, and carry her—while she hit his face with her fists and kicked her legs wildly about—into the bedroom. He flung her down on the bed, then pulled the door shut and turned the key in the lock. Then, pulling off his bathrobe and, standing in his wet trunks, he fumbled with the latter until they had dropped to the floor. He stood, wiry, his prick superbly erect and swollen, broad of shaft, with dark blue veins throbbingly surging against the taut skin. The meatus was plum-shaped, and the lips puckered and twitched in the violent erotic stimulus that goaded him to this incestuous subjugation.

Phyllis huddled into a little ball, drawing her knees up against her panting bosom, her eyes enormous as they stared at the bludgeon meant to batter down the walls of her maiden temple. "Oh please don't, Larry! I'll never forgive you if you try it! You'll hurt me, I don't want you to! It's sinful, you know it is, for a fellow with his own relative! My gosh, if you're that hard up, why don't you jack off?"

"Ah ha!" he exultantly laughed as he strode toward the bed, his cock bobbing with every step. "You're not quite the little innocent you play at being, are you, Phyl? Admit you've played with your pussy lots of times when you've been in bed, thinking of Dan and the other guys you've got a yen for!'

"Please don't, you'll be sorry! Oh gosh, why don't you go out and get a whore? I'm sure you wouldn't have any trouble, there must be houses in a country like this," she babbled.

"Uh-uh. No thanks. I don't want any of those.

Besides, it's you I want to fuck, not any whore. Now either you're going to take it nice and easy, and we'll both have some fun, or I'll rip that suit off and really give it to you, Cuz. Take your choice."

She couldn't believe it was her own sweet familiar Larry talking. She lay there huddled up, panting, her eyes enormous, watching the sturdy young male hurry to the closet, draw out his suitcase, squat down and then stand up with a little white packet clutched in his right hand. "I told you you won't have to worry, baby," he was saying as he came towards the bed again, hastily tearing open the packet. "I'm going to use a safe. It'll be nice, you'll see. It'll be a lot better than your finger."

"Oh don't don't! Oh help me, don't let him oh no, stay away from me no, you're tearing my suit help—ahrr—mffff—ooouuuuhhhohh!"

He had fallen upon her, and had ripped her bathing suit off. Phyllis struck at him, trying to huddle herself into a ball so that he couldn't get at her. But, mockingly, Lawrence began to tickle her and when she wriggled and twisted to one side, he was on her in a flash, mounted over her, his prick digging at the soft thick dark brown fleece of her cunt, while his left hand grasped both of hers. Then, clenching his right fist, he snarled. "Are you going to come across, Phyl, or do I have to smack you?"

Tears blinded her dilated eyes. She whimpered: "Don't hurt me, don't hurt me Larry, I—I'll let you, only don't hurt me, please!"

"That's better, Cuz. Now open those legs and open those hands of yours, because if anybody gets smacked, it's going to be you," he commanded.

Subjugated, trembling, the naked girl resigned herself. Twisting her face to one side, and sobbing wholeheartedly, Phyllis Valery put her palms down against the rumpled cover of the bed, and closed her eyes, aban-

Passion In Rio

doning herself. Beside her, her cousin crouched, panting and shuddering, as he rolled the prophylactic carefully over his swollen prick. Then, a moment of compassion took hold of him, seeing Phyllis abandoned there, legs straddled, body offered in resignation, her face twisted away from him, her eyes closed, her naked breasts rising and falling in a violent upheaval of fear and terror and shame and, also, an iota of sensual curiosity.

"Aw, gee, Phyl, don't take on like that, it's not the end of the world. Once you get me into you, you'll feel how good it is. I told you, it's lots better than with a finger. I'm gonna show you, Phyl honey," he said solicitously, his voice thick and breaking with lust. He put his hands on her bare knees, bent his head and suddenly Phyllis uttered a cry and raised her head to stare at him, a look of surprise on her lovely saucy face. Her own cousin had just kissed her cunt, his lips and tongue saluting that threshold of virginal delight.

"Oh no—what are you doing to me—oh don't, oh hurry and get it over with, before I lose my mind," she hoarsely whispered.

But he didn't answer. His face was thrust against her mound, and he kept kissing and tonguing her pussy until, despite herself, Phyllis began to squirm and twist her buttocks, to arch herself up, to jerk up and about this way and that as the slow, cumulative and lascivious sensations began to permeate her nervous system.

"Now, how's that, Phyl?" he muttered. "Am I hurting you?"

"No-no...but oh you shouldn't...it's awful...I'm your cousin, don't you understand, Larry? If you have to f-fuck, why don't you get a girl here in Rio, somebody you'll never see again, and I promise I won't tell! I swear I won't, if you'll just let me go!"

"No chance, baby. You just lie still there and take it if you know what's good for you." And, once again his mouth set down against her cunt, and now he began to suck until Phyllis could no longer hold back the whimpering little sobs that rose from her as she felt herself drawn inexorably and involuntarily towards the brink of the abyss of carnal desire.

The dainty nodule of her clitoris began to throb and rigidify, for she had masturbated in secret for several years, and she was at once highly sensitized to the tactile sensations her cousin's mouth and tongue were procuring for her. And gradually this attenuation of her resistance, thanks to her own secret precocity in passion, was what undid her and let him conquer her as he had so long lusted to do.

Her head fell back, and the pulse in the soft milky curve of her neck began to hammer violently, while her naked breasts rose and fell with an even more erratic cadence. Now his tongue was gouging against her love-button, and Phyllis could not prevent the flexing spasms which raced up and down her thighs, made her hips jerk sporadically, and made her entire body seem as if it were aflame.

But by now her cousin could no longer hold back the savage urge to couple with that lovely, deliciously rounded, nubile naked body, flesh of his own flesh, blood of his own blood; indeed, the lure of this incestuous cohesion vastly augmented his blind rut. He knelt up, his face a mask of lust, flushed and perspiring, eyes glistening, lips moist and trembling with the infernal desire that possessed him. He could see the pink twitching lips of his cousin's pussy, which he had brought to this state by his own dalliance. The sight drove away his last twinge of conscience, and made him ruthless with his desire. He flung himself down upon her, and Phyllis shrieked as she realized now that he was in earnest, and that now there would be no reprieve for her virgin cunt.

His throbbing organ buried itself between the wet,

Passion In Rio

gaping lips of her vulva, thrust forward till it met the obstruction of her cherry, while Phyllis dug her fingernails into his armpits and twisted this way and that, trying to unsaddle him. But in vain.

With a single thrust, he hurled himself against her hymeneal seal, and Phyllis uttered a shriek which he stifled with the palm of his left hand. She struck at him, trying to push him off, but it was too late. Even as she tried to clench her thighs against his command, he felt himself pierce through the membrane and lodged the very hilt of his prick-length inside her tight narrow cunt.

"Oh no—you're hurting me, oh, Larry, Larry, what have you done to me? You filthy horrible beast, you'll see, I'm going to tell," she wailed. But she got no farther. His mouth came down hard on hers to silence her protest into an ineffectual sputter. Both hands grasped her wrists, and forced her arms out and across the rumpled bed. He luxuriated to feel himself tightly gripped to the very end of his length, and he lingered there as he felt the pulsations of her pussy activating themselves against this unwanted intruder.

"Are you gonna be nice now and let me screw you, Phyl, or do I have to work you over some?" he gasped as he lifted his mouth from hers. Great tears ran down her cheeks, as she twisted her face away and closed her eyes again, whimpering, "I can't, you're too strong for me—but oh, please hurry up and finish it, I hate you, you're filthy and horrible and I don't recognize you, Larry—get it over with then!"

He exhaled a long sigh of delight. And then slowly he began to fuck her, placing his left palm under her buttocks, his right hand cupping her left breast, his mouth pouring kisses over her throat and chin and lips and cheeks and eyes. But the rapid friction began to have its insidious effect upon the lovely naked young girl.

He had already divined that though she might be a

virgin, she was far from being prudishly circumspect. What he had seen through that peephole had told him otherwise. But even Phyllis herself could not fathom the potential of her own woman-threshold as it received this new, probing and distending sensation which his prick caused as it went back and forth inside her tight young sheath.

She was beyond resistance now, beyond recrimination, even. Her eyes were closed and tears continued to edge under the fluttering lids, but the erratic swell of her bare breasts, the convulsive jerks her naked hips gave as he drew himself back to the brink of her pussylips, and then the long moaning sigh she exhaled when he thrust himself back to the hilt inside her cunt, proved only too well that he had taken the upper hand over her and dominated her beyond all hope of self-extrication.

In one of her convulsive twisting, her bare buttocks rubbed against his forefinger. As he thrust himself to the hilt inside her, his forefinger found its way along that sinuous, narrow crease between her milky bottom-globes, and Phyllis uttered a cry as she felt the tip of his forefinger prod the crinkly, dainty, tender rosette of her virgin asshole.

Before she could protest, his finger had inserted itself just inside the ring of protective sphincter muscles. He was wild with excitement as he felt rectal walls clamp and grind against his finger, just as her vaginal sheath was doing against his imbedded cock.

She shuddered furiously again as he drew himself back, only to cram home to the balls, and at the same time his fingers burrowed almost to the hilt inside her quaking bottom-groove. It was too much. With a sobbing groan, Phyllis flung her arms around his neck and her mouth crushed against his as she gave himself up to the amoral ecstasy of physical union.

Alice Valery had managed to get to Benito's room

Passion In Rio

without the old landlady seeing her. She was on his bed now, dressed in only her girdle and stockings, for he had just removed her bra and was busy kissing her still magnificently firm full breasts. Her face was scarlet, and her eyes were closed, but her fingers ruffled his hair as he cradled his head on her swelling bosom. Against her eager cunt, she could feel his hard young prick rubbing this way and that, not yet entering, teasing-torturing her with the most thrilling sensations she had known since her husband had gone to his grave.

"Oh, Benito, I love you so, oh do it to me, I need it, I need it, darling," Alice Valery moaned.

Alice Valery offered herself in joy and rapture, inwardly saying a prayer of gratitude for this handsome Brazilian youth who had brought her back from the edge of the grave into a renewed awareness of her womanhood. As she felt him thrust hesitantly into her, her dream of the other day came true and she reached up and grabbed him and pulled him down upon her, locking her legs over his thighs, arching herself up until she could feel the last inch of that rigid spear he was thrusting into her. Her mouth glued to his, her eyes closed, she inwardly rejoiced that she was being brought back to life as a woman, which she had feared would never again happen after Daniel's untimely death. She wasn't playing housewife to her husband's traveling salesman, or saucy French maid. Now she was getting plowed by a hung Brazilian stud, and loving it. She loved having a dark hard prick in her again, and if it was attached to the taut torso of some young *Carioca*, who cared? He was pleasing her as Daniel never had, making the walls of her cunt sweat with love juice. She wanted Benito more than life itself right now and from experience, she knew that someone this young could fuck her all night.

-11-

Lorna Destry was very dubious about the arrangements her young Brazilian lover, Carlos Nuncialto, had made, but he had assured her repeatedly that all Landau wanted her to do was to pose in some rather curious bondage positions. It was his particular hobby, Carlos glibly explained and nothing at all would happen, and the money the two of them would get from Lorna's willingness to go through with this deal would make it possible for her to stay here in Rio with him. Lorna Destry couldn't see through the suave cynicism of the teenaged bellboy. All she knew was that for the first time in her life she was truly loved and that at any cost she wanted to be with Carlos forever. He didn't think she was ugly, he wasn't like that horrible bastard back in Miami. He thought she was beautiful and that she had a magnificent body and he had shown it too, in the way he had made love to her. She felt like a young girl who couldn't get enough. In fact, she really didn't want to leave Carlos at all this afternoon, though the *Senhor* Landau had asked that she come to his house in a cab and be there about four thirty.

She was wearing only her slip, and she didn't care at all that it was ruffled up above her belly. Carlos, very athletic, with that coffee-colored skin of his and those rippling muscles, was seated on the edge of the bed wearing only his undershirt and socks. His limp cock dangled to one side on his thigh and he absentmindedly

Passion In Rio

scratched himself on the hip. He was thinking of the money. The masked ball of the Copacabana Palace would start about nine o'clock tonight, and that ticket was being held for him just until six. He would have to get this *gringa* bitch over to the *Senhor* Landau as fast as he could, get his money, and hurry back to Porfirio, and after that he would have to take the ticket to Tianha, along with the costume he had gone ahead and bought for her. In a way he felt like crying because he wanted to be there with her and to see her in that wonderful mermaid costume and then, after the ball, take her to his room and fuck her. She would have to say yes now, after accepting a ticket to the most exclusive ball in all Rio—not to mention that wonderful costume. She wasn't going to put him off any longer.

"Darling?"

"What is it?" he said very crossly. Lorna's face at once crumpled, and tears sprang to her eyes. This wasn't the tender, wonderfully romantic lover of their passionate night. She hadn't believed he could be so harsh. But perhaps he was tired, the darling. There was certainly excuse enough for that, considering how many times he had done it to her. She blushed to think about it. But the sight of his limp cock filled her with a new kind of ecstatic longing. She reached out gently and touched his thigh, an inch away from where the tip of his prick lay in drooping abandon. "Carlos? You do love me, don't you?"

"Of course I do, Lorna, but you see, don't you, how important it is for you to do this for me? I'm a bellboy and I don't make too much money at the hotel. I need you, my beautiful one. Nobody would pay me to pose, not even a men's magazine, but this crazy turista, he'll pay so much money that we can be together for a long time. And I'm going to talk to some of my friends about getting you a job here and also extending your visa. You do want to stay with me, don't you, Lorna?"

"Oh, Carlos, you know I do, you know I do! Oh darling won't you love me one last time before I have to leave?"

"We'd better not, really. When you come back, I'll make it up to you," he assured her. He turned to her now and bent and kissed her pussy. Lorna uttered a soft moaning cry and spread her thighs wantonly, tilting her head back and closing her eyes. "Oh, take me, Carlos, just one last time before I go there! Please take me, it'll give me courage!"

The brilliant sun was filtering through the drawn blinds at the top where they were badly frayed and in need of repair. They cast a rather stark, glaring pattern on her face, and Carlos grimaced with distaste. That angular, almost bony face with the blotches of acne. Stay with this for the rest of his young life? No thank you! Not when he had a piece like Tianha, so marvelously made, with such an insolent tantalizing face. But then, he didn't dare let this stupid woman know what was really going to happen to her, and it really didn't matter once the *Senhor* Landau got her. Porfirio had told him that there might be a little whipping but everyone knew that a woman needed to be whipped and once she got it, sexy as she was because she had been neglected so long, she'd be just as randy for *Senhor* Landau as she was for him and she wouldn't even miss him. And she didn't dare go to any law authority and complain about him because there would be ways of punishing her, and besides she couldn't prove a thing. So he'd give her few more minutes of fun. He wouldn't get to Tianha until very early Sunday morning, and maybe even then she would be drunk on the champagne she would drink at the masked ball.

"I do love you *querida*," he murmured. He bent

Passion In Rio

down and gave her pussy another long and exquisitely tantalizing kiss, pressing the tip of his tongue right into the center of her groove. Lorna uttered a sobbing groan and wriggled closer, yawning her thighs until they nearly split apart in her eagerness to give all of herself to her lover. He shrugged his shoulders. The things one had to do to get what one wanted! Oh well, might as well humor the bitch. He clambered onto the bed and knelt at her side, watched her as she reached out to fondle his cock, blushing like a silly schoolgirl who had just had her first kiss. Who would have thought that this sharp-faced *gringa* would want it so badly? Though he had to admit that it hadn't been too bad. She really had lovely long legs that could lock around him tightly when she fucked. But they were nothing like Tianha's.

"You see, Carlos? You do want me again, you know you do!" Lorna Destry gasped with delight as she felt his cock stiffen under the manipulations of her fingers. And when he sank down upon her she clutched him desperately as a drowning man clutches at a cork upon the ocean, for he was her only chance for happiness.

He coddled her and cajoled her amply and she was almost in a happy mood after taking a bath and putting on makeup and dressing to take a cab to the house of the *Senhor* Landau. He told her that he would ride along with her in the cab to give her courage, and that he would call the man himself tonight to see how everything went. He would be waiting for her and she was to come back to his room as soon as it was over.

And so Lorna Destry, a waitress from Miami, rode in a cab that studiously avoided the main streets, which were already crowded with cheering happy people. She was enroute to the most horrifying experience of her entire life…yet one which, as destiny would show, had its purpose in the scheme of things and the cause of justice for vicious evils wrought upon the helpless and the innocent.

"Now you go right up the walk and ring the doorbell, *querida*," he told her. "I'll come along with you and stand out there until I know everything's all right. You see? I told you, it's only a few pictures. And what does it matter if someone else sees your beautiful body? He won't have it, not the way I have. And we'll be together again, as soon as it's over, remember?"

"Oh yes, my dearest Carlos, my lover, my sweet boy!" Lorna Destry cooed. She squeezed his hand, took a long deep breath, and went up the steps to the elegant house. She pushed the doorbell and waited and looked back at Carlos who waved to her, standing off in the garden, near a stone statue of a nymph kneeling by a fawn, her arm about its neck. The door swung open and Amelia, the handsome housekeeper from Curaçao, confronted Lorna Destry. She wore a black satin dress, high-necked, the skirt hem descending to midcalf, and her face was grave and somber. "Yes?" she curtly asked.

"I-I have an appointment with the *Senhor* Landau," Lorna Destry answered. She glanced nervously back and Carlos again waved to her.

"I know," Amelia interrupted. "Follow me, please."

She led Lorna Destry down a narrow hallway that seemed to skirt the living room, which Lorna could see was concealed with heavy velvet drapes. At the end of the corridor, she opened a little door and waited, gesturing for Lorna to go downstairs. There was a narrow stone stairway, but there was an electric light on the wall inside which illuminated the way. Lorna Destry had a moment's hesitation. "But I thought the *Senhor* Landau would receive me."

"Of course, *Senhora*," Amelia said impatiently, her tone one of annoyance. "He is waiting for you down there. I am to take you to him."

"Oh, all right," Lorna Destry began to descend the narrow stone steps. The sound of her heels on the stone

Passion In Rio

filled her with a kind of inexplicable presentiment. When she found herself at the bottom of the stairway, a magnificently beautiful red-haired woman stood facing her. It was Marguerite Villefrance, the mistress of Gottfried von Arnheim. The former Nazi concentration camp commandant had told his sultry red-haired mistress that he wished her to aid him in a most amusing little game. It would be a game in which she might play an important role if she so desired. And when he had intimated what this game was, the sensual Marguerite had gasped with delight, and whispered. "Mon cher, but didn't you know all this time that I've always had a mania for whipping a pretty girl? You'll see how nice I'll be in bed tonight after I have thrashed her well for you. Who is she?"

"Some American bitch who got herself involved with a bellboy, that's all. It doesn't matter who she is, Liebling," he said, patting her on the bottom. He had decided to tell her about his little penchant to involve her, and once she showed herself to be sadistically inclined towards Lorna Destry, he would turn the tables very cleverly on her in turn and have two very delectable victims to torture at the same time. It would be just like the old happy days at the camp! And after that, he would make both of them aid him in enslaving the haughty housekeeper, Amelia.

"Is this where I'm supposed to pose?" Lorna Destry naively asked.

"Of course it is. Come along with me. *Senhor* Landau has been expecting you for quite some time. I'll take you to him." Marguerite smilingly extended her hand and grasped Lorna Destry's wrist.

Outside, Carlos Nuncialto had gone down the sidewalk to the left of the elegant mansion and there met the bald, paunchy, ex-Nazi who handed him a sheaf of bills, clapped him on the back and told him if he even found another girl who was suitable, to keep in touch. Carlos had kept the cab waiting, and hurried back to it now so that he could pay Porfirio for the ticket. Then he would keep the same cab and get to Tianha. As they cab pulled away from the Nazi's house he thought of Lorna. "Stupid bitch," he said with a smile, then his prick began to ache at the thought of the gratitude lovely Tianha would show him.

Marguerite Villefranche led Lorna Destry towards a heavy gray metal door, turned the knob, pushed the door open and then suddenly thrust Lorna inside. The quick movement had caught the girl so by surprise that she uttered a cry and stumbled forward and fell flat on her belly. The door clanged shut behind her. As she raised her eyes, Lorna Destry uttered a cry of stupefaction.

It might have been a medieval dungeon. It was windowless, and on the walls were panoplies of terrifying instruments: Iron pincers and tongs, whips of all descriptions, manacles, a kind of helmet with a metal bit—a replica, only even more ingeniously made, of the kind of "scold bridle" which the Pilgrim fathers used to apply on sharp-tongued woman. But this was not all that made her blood curdle with horror. In one corner of the room stood a sinister wooden rack with a windlass at each end, so that the arms or the legs or both might be tractioned, as the executioner desired. Opposite, there was a St. Andrew's cross with metal gyves fixed into the wood at each of the four extremities. Across the room stood a pillory, and to one side of it as sharp-ridged wooden saw horse to whose legs there were attached buckling straps.

"Where is—where is," Lorna faltered as she righted herself.

"He'll be along presently," Marguerite snapped. "Come on now, take off your clothes and get all naked.

You were told what your assignment was, weren't you?"

"I-I was told I was to pose for pictures of b-bondage," Lorna Destry stammered.

"And so you will. But hurry now, he'll be very cross if you aren't naked by the time he comes here," the sultry woman commanded.

Blushing furiously under Marguerite's amused glance, Lorna Destry took all her clothes off and was naked. She bit her lips and blushed again as she saw Marguerite's dark-blue eyes leave her body, and as she stood on her bare feet on the cold stone floor, she began to regret her impulsiveness.

There was the sound of a key turning in the lock, the door swung open, and Gottfried von Arnheim entered. He wore black leather tights around his plump bottom and gusseting in between the legs there was a silver zipper at the front of the tights, like the fly on a pair of trousers. He wore black leather boots to the knees, boots with spurs made of fine silver, and black gloves to the elbow. His fat hairy body was repugnant to Lorna Destry, and she uttered a cry and clapped her hands against her pussy while she tried to shield her breasts with the other arm.

"Is everything in readiness, my dear Marguerite?" he blandly asked.

The woman nodded. "She took a little time to undress, but as you see, I convinced her."

"Thank you, darling. Now let's see how we begin. I think perhaps with the pillory."

"Just as you say, dearest," Marguerite told her perverse lover. Approaching the naked Lorna, she seized the latter by the elbow and hissed. "Come along now, don't keep him waiting! You'll be sorry if you do. We'll take the photographs right away and then it'll be over for you." This somewhat reassured the girl and she let herself be pushed along to the pillory. Marguerite deftly opened the mechanism, drew up the upper portion, and Lorna meekly bowed her head and extended her arms so that when the upper portion was drawn down and locked into place her wrists and neck were tightly imprisoned as if in a vise.

Von Arnheim had already showed his beautiful mistress how to operate some of the mechanisms. It amused him to think that after two years of fucking this haughty beauty who had been quite a prize to attain, he had suddenly discovered that she was a sadist too. What a laugh it would be on her when she found that he was even more of one and that he intended to make her his victim along with this long-legged American bitch. The girl didn't have too much of a face, but one had to give her credit for a beautiful pair of Butzen and a magnificent Arsch!

"Take the feather, Marguerite my love," he said in a thickening voice, "And tickle her nipples and in between her legs a little while I warm her up on the other side."

"What—what are you going to do to me? Aren't you going to take pictures?" Lorna cried in a hoarse voice as she began to struggle in her bonds. But the heavy pillory did not release her by so much as an inch, and all she did was to chafe her neck and wrists as she struggled. Moreover, she found that she was standing almost on tiptoe, which put a painful strain on all her muscles.

Gottfried von Arnheim strode over to the wall and, deliberating a long moment, licked his lips with relish as he took down a five-thonged red leather martinet with a short wooden handle. The finely worked leather had been polished and soaked in oil, and its tip ended in notched ends to impart additional sting.

He slowly walked back to the helpless naked woman, and, taking his place to her left, dangled the thongs to the floor as he studied her squirming body. She really

Passion In Rio

had wonderful legs, and doubtless a few good cuts up between them would really make her dance and beg for mercy! He would pretend that she was a Czech bitch, like that Karin Dovrov whom he had personally interrogated in the next to the last year of the war which the Third Reich ought to have won. He had been trying to find out the names and the headquarters of the Czech underground and Karin Dovrov had refused to give them to him. He'd begun by giving her a good and playful spanking, just to humiliate her, for she had been a beautiful and educated woman in her twenties, the fiancee of a very important Czech newspaper editor. And then after the spanking, he'd used a whip on her breasts and belly and finally up between her legs until she had finally told him everything he had wanted to know. He'd had a lovely weekend fucking and buggering her until she had finally been stood up against the wall and used for bayonet practice.

Marguerite took off her long cocktail frock as she stood opposite poor Lorna Destry at the pillory. Lorna uttered a cry to discover that the French beauty was naked under the frock except for her high-heeled pumps. She had pear-shaped breasts that stuck out boldly, a suave belly, beautifully supple long legs, and a pale milky skin exquisitely flecked with rose tones. In her hand she held a long white egret plume, and with this she began to tickle Lorna's nipples. Lorna gasped and groaned and twisted, stammering embarrassed phrases. "Oh don't please—what are you doing—why doesn't he take the pictures—don't do that to me—it's shameful!"

And then suddenly she uttered a maddened cry as the five thongs of the martinet wrapped around her naked bottom cheeks. She lunged forward, the pillory creaking with her effort, and then a second cut and a third curled the biting thongs over her oval-cheeked posterior, while Marguerite, giggling insanely, began to rub the feather against the victim's cunt.

Now in the room one could hear only the hoarse breathing and grunting of the Nazi sadist, the sensual giggling of Marguerite Villefranche and the agonized despairing cries of the betrayed Lorna Destry, whose body leaped and jerked under the lashes of the martinet and whose flesh began to redden with the angry stripes the expert flagellant imparted to it.

Carnival '60 had begun for Gottfried von Arnheim.

-12-

Miguel Valdes had made a last-minute switch in his costume for the Carnival, and when he reported Sunday evening to Lorenzo Bivilar, the leader of the *escola*, which he had the honor of representing, the latter scowled at him. "What the devil made you change to that, of all things, hombre?" the plump, mustachioed, bespectacled Lorenzo growled. He was the head of a stationery shop of the Calle do Azucar and very proud of the sales quota he had set the past three months. His boss, who owned three such shops in the business district of Rio, had promised to contribute an extra prize if the *escola* received favorable mention in the newspaper for its float, an elaborate representation of a *Carioca* girl clad in only a bikini and holding a parasol, with a cockatoo perched on each shoulder, sitting on a floral cornucopia and throwing blossoms to the spectators, a float to be drawn by two white horses with collars of flowers and reins of pure white satin sewn with silver cloth.

Miguel passed it off as a great joke. "You see, *jefe*," he wheedlingly explained, "where I work as a night porter at the Trocadero, everybody is snooping in the storage room and saying, 'Miguel, do this!' and 'Miguel, do that!' It is as if I had policemen all around me. So, *jefe*, I decided for the Carnival to be a policeman myself. Where is the harm in it?"

"Go along with you, man, and take your place in the processional," Lorenzo grumbled.

Miguel Valdes uttered a sigh of relief. He had managed in a costume shop half a mile from the hotel where he worked to find an ancient Keystone Cop costume, complete with the outrageous hat, the shiny brass buttons, and the exaggerated night stick. He wore a black mask over his eyes and nose, and he had added a false Van Dyke beard to his chin. It was most imposing. And this way he would be able to watch his lovely young Miranda in her Gypsy costume pairing off with the conniving bastard, Francisco da Rucosta.

It couldn't have been a more beautiful night for a parade, and Miguel treated himself to a glass of cachaca to give himself courage for what he meant to do. He had a belt and pistol holster, and of course the gun fired blanks and it was one of those huge guns with a long barrel which looked comical to begin with. He had made a particular point of firing the gun one or two times before Lorenzo, just to prove to the leader of the *escola* that these bullets were really blanks. And then he had reloaded. But the last bullet was a real bullet—and it was meant for the black heart of Francisco da Rucosta.

Lovely young Miranda had been most mysterious this afternoon. She had pouted at him and told him that he had been a very bad boy and not bought her a nice present for the Carnival. So just for that, she said, she wasn't going to go with him. His eyebrows had arched and he had a knowing smile on his face as he said, "Ah, so that's it, is it?"

To which she had tartly retorted, "You're acting like a child, Miguel! And you are also acting like an old man, which isn't good at all for a young girl like me. You've been a good husband, and even a good lover, but lately you've been treating me as if I were a bad girl, a bad daughter. I don't like it one little bit, I can tell you that. So that's why you're going to the Carnival with

Passion In Rio

your *escola* ahead of me. I'm not so sure I'm even going. But if I do go, I'll go by myself and I'll flirt all I like and there's nothing you can do about it. Until next Wednesday, this is the Carnival, Miguel. I'm going to punish you for treating me with such nasty suspicions."

Well it had been a good act, he told himself. Let her do what she wanted. Let her come late if that was her little whim, but he would be there and he would see, later on, whom she paired off with. And then, amid all the cheering and the blowing of horns and the playing of the bands, nobody would hear a shot. And Francisco da Rucosta wouldn't be around to bother other men's wives any longer. And if anybody said anything to him, he would just act horrified and of course he wouldn't understand how a live bullet could have got into the box of blanks he had brought at such and such a shop.

He'd taken great pains to buy that box at a shop where he wasn't known and to which he had cleverly taken a friend as a witness in case he might need one. He had made a point of asking the old shopkeeper whether there was any danger that maybe one or two of the bullets might really be live after all. The shopkeeper had laughed and told him that if he found a live bullet, he was to come back to the shop and he would get a free box of blanks in return. Of course, that night, he'd carefully put a live bullet along the top row and this was the bullet which was the last in the chamber.

But when the parade began, Miguel Valdes momentarily forgot his hatred for the handsome young assistant manager of the restaurant at the Trocadero. It was really a wonderful Carnival. A beautiful soft balmy night, the moon was out and the stars as well, and the confetti and the fireworks and the bands and the spectators cheering. They liked his float, and that made him proud to be a member of this escola. And maybe after the disagreeable part of the Carnival was finished with, he might find himself a cute little *Carioca*, a girl who wanted to have a fling before she went back to work. Maybe some pretty secretary at one of the electrical firms, or a manicurist in one of the many beauty shops. He might even take her to the famous Bec Fin Restaurant to celebrate getting rid of a rival and making a conquest all in the same night.

His *escola* was turning around the *Avenida Rio Bravo*, past the National Museum of Fine Arts, and he was strutting along, waving his nightstick and covertly watching the luscious thighs of a tall red-haired beauty who was wearing a cheongsam, a mask, and a silver-blonde wig. It was a bit too short in back, so he saw that she had natural red hair, lustrous and coppery. And what smooth, satiny coffee-colored skin to go with it! She had on high-heeled pumps, and she was practically six feet tall in them, and the way her bottom wiggled made him conscious that though Miranda said he was an old man, he was still strong enough to service a piece like this one any night in the week. The cheongsam was slashed very high, and he could see bare skin and just the outline of the gauziest part of white nylon panties. He wished that he hadn't been so cross with Miranda. But then, if she'd been a good wife and not tried to deceive him with that handsome swine, they could have had a little supper late tonight and then rented a room in one of the hotels and pretended to be lovers meeting for the first time and what a wonderful, glorious fuck they could have had.

The girl in the silver-blonde wig glanced back at him and gave him a wink through the slits of her mask. He licked his lips. Maybe when this was all over, he could proposition her. She would really give him a workout, with that luscious pair of bottom-cheeks and those wonderful long legs. She was even prettier than Miranda.

And then he saw Miranda far ahead of him, Miranda

in her Gypsy costume and beside her a man with a black Venetian face mask, wearing the costume of a Roman centurion: helmet, breast plate, buskins and sandals, a short wooden sword tucked into his belt, and his right arm was around Miranda's waist. The fellow had black hair, with pomade on it. That could only be Francisco da Rucosta!

The cheering of the spectators was deafening as the girl on the cornucopia passed by. Miguel Valdes began to move forward, leaving his position and breaking ranks to catch up with his faithless wife. As he went by, he brushed against the girl in the silver-blonde wig and muttered. "Patience, my beauty, I'll see you after parade. How about a little supper and some fun?" And she'd said haughtily, *"Va embota, chamarei um guarda!"*

Well, she could go to hell too! There'd be another woman, never mind. Even a little whore would be welcome tonight, by way of celebrating what he was going to do. It wouldn't take very long. They were about three rows ahead of him, and Miguel Valdes slyly opened his holster and drew out the gun. He raised it in the air and fired two shots. He swung his nightstick with the other hand and gesticulated towards the crowd. They cheered him, finding him hilarious. It was going to be so easy!

Of course he had to be sure. Now he was close enough to see Miranda's body. No mistaking it, no mistaking those long legs, and there were the imitation gold earrings and the sparkling tiara and the Gypsy costume. Unmistakably, it was Miranda. And that dirty little bitch was turning her head to look at the Roman centurion.

He fired two more shots in the air. One more, and the sixth and last would be the live bullet. He made more gestures with the nightstick, pretended to move back and forth, crouching down as if to detect a criminal. He was rewarded with cheers again. He straightened, stepped back, lifted his gun and fired again in the air, and once again a roar of laughter rewarded his pantomime.

And now he knew exactly what he had to do. He ran up close until he was abreast of Miranda, whose face was hidden by a mask, and he lifted the nightstick in his left hand and pretended to strike down on the helmet of the centurion. At the same time, he aimed the gun in his right hand at the middle of Francisco da Rucosta's back and pulled the trigger.

The centurion stumbled, walked another pace or two, and went down to his knees. Suddenly the cheering had stopped, and the people behind Miguel had halted. For a terrible instant, a deathly silence seemed to encompass all of this little tableau. And then the centurion turned his face, groped for his mask with a trembling hand and ripped it away.

Miguel Valdes uttered a shriek of horror. It wasn't Francisco da Rucosta. It was a man he had never seen before. And Miranda—

"What have you done? Assassin! You've killed my husband! You demon, you murderer! And he's a policeman—a real policeman, stop him, stop him!" the girl shrieked.

It wasn't Miranda. It was a girl who wore a costume identical to Miranda's. And now that she had the mask off, Miguel Valdes stood there rooted to the pavement, for it was Lucetta Caimo, Miranda's best friend, and the man he had killed could have been her husband Frederico.

He let the gun drop from his nerveless fingers, and then two men from his own *escola* seized him by the shoulders and dragged him over towards the sidewalk, striking him with their fists, raging at him. But he couldn't understand, he couldn't hear. His mind was numb with the horror of it. He had killed an innocent man.

Passion In Rio

At that very moment, Miranda Valdes and Francisco de Rucosta were lying naked in each other's arms in a little hotel in Sao Paulo. Miranda was saying, "It was such a marvelous idea of yours, my darling Francisco, to have me lend my costume to my dear friend Lucetta. My stupid husband was no doubt kept occupied thinking it was I in the parade all the time. And what a scare I gave him when I told him I was going off by myself. You should have seen his face! He was sure that I was going to meet you!"

Francisco de Rucosta chuckled lazily. One of his hands was on Miranda's bosom, the other was caressing the furry fronds of her pussy, while one of her slim hands toyed with his stiffening cock. They had already fucked twice in the past hour, and they were titillating themselves for a long and leisurely and luxurious finale to their night of love.

"Well, weren't you?" he asked. "I shall hate to leave Rio, that beach and ocean and some of the nice little restaurants, including the one that I helped manage. But then, I've got a much better job at the best hotel in Sao Paulo, and you'll take back your maiden name and we can marry and no one will ever find out. I didn't tell my boss where I was going, either. But I've had this offer from my good friend Pablo Baiuca for about six months now, and the time was just perfect for accepting it."

"Why don't you stop talking, darling, and love me hard?" Miranda murmured as her fingers tensed against his prick. With a salacious little chuckle, Francisco rolled over on top of her and, thrusting himself deep into her warm moist cleft, slid his hands under her jouncy buttocks and began to fuck the wife of a murderer.

-13-

Kay Arnold knew that she had to make a play for Joanne Claremont as quickly as possible, because on Thursday, the day after the Carnival, they'd go back to New York and she'd never get another chance. Having had so long-retained a passion for the honey-haired young designer, Kay had been unusually continent, considering her furious lesbian penchants. And so on this Sunday afternoon, when Joanne proposed that they have an early supper and go out to the street to watch the parade of the escolas, Kay readily assented. But she made a counter-proposal: "Let's have a swim right after lunch, and then take a nap and have our supper and we'll be fresh. The water is so beautiful out there, and you know we won't get another chance back in New York."

"Fine," Joanne agreed. Kay went into the bathroom and put on her skintight bathing suit and came out, preening herself, cupping her breasts and giving Joanne a lazy smile. "Like my suit, honey?"

"It's very nice, Kay. Now I'll go put on mine."

"Can I help you with anything, honey?" Kay could not quite keep the urgent note of desire out of her voice.

Joanne Claremont gave her roommate a wondering look, then shook her head. "I'm a big girl now, Kay. I can undress myself quite nicely, thanks."

"I-I didn't mean that the way it sounded, Joanne,"

Passion In Rio

Kay floundered. "I wish you wouldn't get into a huff whenever I try to be nice to you."

But Joanne was remembering what Mathilda Doran had told her just before they had left New York for Rio. She had intimated that Kay was a Sapphist, and Joanne had at first been repelled by that news, and then begun to think about it.

The fact was, although she couldn't bring herself to admit it, that she was getting terribly passionate. The reason for that, of course, was her absence from her darling David, and she told herself that just as soon as they got back to New York, she would boldly ask him to set as early a date as possible for their marriage. She needed love. This artificial, shallow world of fashion wasn't really for her. And she knew that she had competence as a designer, that she could always sell one of her original ideas to a shop like Mathilda's, doing it freelance even as a housewife. That would be wonderful, supplementing her income in that way, showing David that she was a good wife, and a partner in their union.

All the same, she couldn't take her eyes off Kay's stunning breasts, nor those long legs. And the small red sensual mouth, moistened now and quivering, made her shiver inwardly, though she didn't exactly know why.

So, more troubled than she cared to admit, she went into the bathroom, locked the door and put on her bathing suit, then her robe, and emerged. Kay was smoking a cigarette and sitting on the couch, her beautiful bare legs crossed, the upper leg provocatively waggling back and forth. "You're gorgeous, Joanne," she said. "If I were a man, I'd really go for you. But I go for you anyway, I think you know that."

"Kay—please don't talk like that. You know I'm engaged to David."

"Of course you are, honey. But this is Carnival time down here. All the natives throw away their inhibitions and their stuffy conventions just for these four days. They even starve themselves so that they can dress up in costumes and have a wonderful time and sleep with other men's wives and everything. You know the old proverb, when you're in Rome, do as the Romans do. Well, why don't you just relax for once, until the Carnival is over? If you let yourself go, you won't be taking anything away from David that belongs to him, and I think you'll be a better woman for it. In bed, I mean."

Kay stared at her companion, her heart in her eyes. There. She had gambled everything on one throw of the dice. There wasn't any other way to do it. She didn't want to be sneaky about it, copping a free feel and letting Joanne suddenly get offended. It was better this way, to be direct.

"At least that was very honest," Joanne admitted, and her voice was just the least bit unsteady. "But you see, Kay, I guess I've been brought up all my life to think of marrying a man and going to bed with him. That's what they call normal, I guess. I-I don't even know what it is that girls do when they want to love other girls."

Kay's heart began to pound rapidly now. Her grey-green eyes grew luminous with an eager desire. "I'd like to show you, darling. It's tender and romantic and beautiful. It doesn't at all negate your womanliness, so far as David is concerned, and I don't think you'll be shocked by it. Haven't you ever felt affection for someone other than a man?"

"My mother, of course."

"There's that too, yes. But when you were in high school, didn't you have a gym teacher or maybe a math teacher you were crazy about?"

Joanne Claremont frowned, trying to remember. Kay broke in: "Let's be honest with each other, honey.

There's nothing shameful when it's brought out into the open. I'll admit I've got a real hankering for you. And it's just my nature. I don't like men, I had a bad experience, and I've found tenderness and affection with other women, it's only natural that I should prefer that. But to go back—to be honest now, as I'll be with you. Certainly as a young girl you must have—well, relieved yourself when you had naughty dreams or thoughts, didn't you?"

Joanne's lovely face flamed, and she gulped and looked down at the floor. "I-I suppose so," she faltered.

"Well, honey, the only difference then is that instead of being selfish and doing it to yourself, you do it with someone else who likes you very much, and whom you like in return. Only there's much more to it than just using your finger."

"I-I don't think we ought to go on talking like this, Kay, really I don't," the younger beauty said nervously.

"I just want you to do one thing for me, and that's all. I promise, word of honor, I won't ever try anything again. But in all honesty, darling, do this one thing for me, and you'll answer your own question."

"What is it?"

Kay Arnold patted the couch beside her. "Come sit down next to me and let me kiss you, just once. And you're not to break away or stop me until the one kiss is over. That's all I ask."

Joanne Claremont hesitated, the waves of crimson still flooding her lovely dimpled cheeks. Her eyes rested on Kay's quivering long sleek thighs, and she suddenly felt herself stricken with an inner longing that she couldn't quite define.

"I guess it won't do any harm, just once," she said nervously as she moved over to sit down on the couch. Now it was Kay Arnold's turn to quiver, for the nearness of Joanne, the pressure of their bare thighs, together, and the sight of that magnificent pair of breasts, quickly rising and falling against the tight cut of Joanne's bathing suit, made the lesbian designer nearly swoon with unrequited lust. Nonetheless, she steeled herself to make this first and last attempt succeed by its very warmth. She put her left arm around Joanne's supple waist, her right hand tilting up the young woman's chin, and then very slowly and deliberately she pressed her mouth to the blonde's. Her lips were moist and parted, and she fused them with Joanne's in an ardent and yet gentle and tender union. At the same time, her right hand moved down from Joanne's chin to one round full breast which strained against the tight bodice of the bathing suit and as she prolonged the kiss, her palm lightly touched the nippled crest of that luscious loveglobe.

Joanne Claremont uttered a sigh, languorous and bemused. For a moment she started, her naked thigh pressing convulsively against Kay's, and then her eyes closed and with an inarticulate little moan, she flung her arms around Kay Arnold and gave back kiss for passionate kiss.

Inside her pussy there was an itching and tingling that had become overpowering. The moist sweet fruit of Kay Arnold's expert mouth had seduced her, ravished her as assuredly as if David himself had been titillating her erogenous zones.

The svelte lesbian uttered a little cry of triumphant delight when she felt her victim capitulate. Now her hand boldly cupped the swelling breast, and her tongue delicately flicked between Joanne's trembling lips to brush the girl's tongue and to add that subtle goad of Sapphic desire to the conquest of this tasty virgin who was at the threshold of yearning womanhood.

Now their thighs pressed tightly together and Joanne Claremont experienced the indescribable longing of

Passion In Rio

flesh-to-flesh communion, became aware of her own churning senses, as a woman who longed for complete fulfillment. In turn, one of her own hands falteringly moved towards Kay's bosom, hesitantly grazing it, as the delighted lesbian nodded and pressed herself even more tightly against her partner. Her left hand slipped down to stroke Joanne's firm rounded hips, savoring the resilient flesh through the thin snug suit. And then, at last, her right hand made its progression down that suave belly towards the abdomen and thence to Joanne Claremont's loin. Her fingertips pressing ever so delicately against the rim of the virgin vulva.

Joanne Claremont whimpered, instinctively clutching her naked thighs, her eyes closing, her nostrils flickering with rapture and anguish commingled. Her body had become a temple of furious and diametrically opposed sensations now. She felt herself arch her loins towards Kay's fingers, begging for that salacious, readying caress.

And now her own tongue ventured forth in quest of Kay's, and as it met the lesbian's she experienced an electrifying shock through all her being, which completely annihilated her last reserve, her final doubt and inhibition.

She fell back swooning on the couch, her breasts rising and falling violently, half turned lovely bare legs dangling from the edge of the couch onto the floor. The muscles of her naked calves rippled and flexed voluptuously as Kay's eyes glistened at the sight of this delicious morsel of femininity on the point of complete and irrevocable surrender. Her forefinger now probed between the lips of Joanne Claremont's virgin snatch, pressing the thin satiny material of the bathing suit into that tender crotch, rasping and frictioning the membrane of the virginal love-citadel. And still her lips locked over the panting mouth, and still her mouth delved ardently between the blonde's parted lips.

Joanne's hand was squeezing Kay's breast, reciprocating as best she knew how, to thank her instructress in this amatory initiation. By now Kay's left hand had reached Joanne's rounded hip and was fondling and kneading it, while she continued the pressure of her right forefinger against Joanne's now moistening and twitching cunt.

"There," she said in a husky, shuddering voice, when at last she broke off that endless kiss. "And now do you find it so repulsive, darling?"

Joanne's eyes opened—the sky-blue irises humid and swimming—as she moaned, "Oh, no! oh, my god, Kay, darling, no! oh, love me, go ahead and love me, show me how! Lick me down there! Lick me all over! Love me now!"

Kay Arnold could hardly contain herself. She had exerted the most violent self-control to keep from ripping off that bathing suit and exposing the tempting, voluptuous young body of this delectable pupil. She took Joanne's hands and guided them to the fasteners at the hips of the bathing suit, so that Joanne herself could participate in this surrender. Then she helped the whimpering young woman work the suit down and off her body, and Joanne Claremont was naked. The dark blonde thicket of pussy hair covered that plump soft lovenook, and Kay's finger again returned to it, but this time to enter the lips and to find the nodule of Joanne's clitoris. This she began to frig, with a very slow and lingering caress, scarcely grazing the tiny pink button that began to stiffen and grow tumescent.

When she saw Joanne's flanks shudder, saw that magnificent bosom rise and fall erratically, she stopped and rose. Swiftly she drew off her suit, and she was naked too.

Passion In Rio

She lifted Joanne's bare legs onto the couch, parting them sweetly as her long slim fingers glided from Joanne's knees almost to the crotch and back again along the tender, exquisitely sensitive surface of the inner thighs. And then as she saw Joanne smile at her, saw Joanne's sky-blue eyes widen with tears and longing, she uttered a cry and flung herself down. At once Joanne's arms and legs accepted her, and Joanne's mouth crushed to Kay's in a perfect paean of rapturous acceptance. Joanne Claremont could feel the rubbing of Kay's breasts on hers, the frictioning of that suave belly on hers, and most of all the tickling of Kay's pussyhair as the lesbian ground her mound back and forth over her victim's.

Now they began to exchange a passionate kiss, in which Joanne Claremont, the uninitiated virgin, gave back more than she derived. Her box was aflame, quivering violently, her nipples stiffened and darkened, her cuntlips moist with the soft cream of her amorous distillation.

Joanne bit her lower lip to keep from crying out in ecstasy. The sensation of Kay's clit rubbing against her own was more than she could bear. She felt as if she might explode, and yet she wanted to prolong the feeling of anticipation. A deep guttural sound vibrated in Kay's throat as she pulled herself up and down the length of Joanne's body.

Kay took one of Joanne's nipple's between her slippery lips and gave it a gentle nip. Joanne gasped at the odd combination of pleasure and pain that it brought her. Kay laughed gently at her reaction.

"Doesn't your darling David ever nibble you, from time to time? No? Well then I guess he probably never does this either."

With that, Kay trailed her tongue down the center of Joanne's torso, careful not to linger in one place too long. When she reached her belly button, she explored it with the pointy tip, causing Joanne to giggle with embarrassment.

"Oh Kay, stop teasing! You're driving me simply mad!" Joanne's protestations were cut short by the throbbing she began to feel between her legs as Kay began an achingly slow descent into her furry triangle.

Joanne held her breath as Kay's tongue continued downward, skipping over her clit and burying itself deeply in her swollen gash. Joanne raised her head for a moment to catch sight of Kay's lovely head bobbing up and down over her mound, her large breasts swinging over her thighs as she moved. The sight of the experienced lesbian furiously licking her cunt brought Joanne perilously close to climaxing. She tensed the muscles in her thighs as if to hold back the flood she felt boiling between her legs.

Sensing her imminent explosion, Kay lifted her head for a moment to catch sight of Joanne's pleasure-wracked face. How beautiful she looks right now, thought Kay. Swinging her hips around, she carefully positioned her glistening snatch above Joanne's mouth. From this angle, she was able to look between their stomachs and see Joanne's tongue snake tentatively out of her mouth toward the hovering pussy. Kay buried her face in Joanne's slit and waited to feel the tongue of the newly initiated woman on her own clit.

Joanne was senseless with desire and showed no repugnance at the offered gift. She plunged her tongue deep inside Kay's hungry cunt, darting in and out slowly and deliberately until she felt her own crisis was upon her. As she felt the spasms take hold of her body, she took Kay's clit between her lips and alternately sucked and caressed the pulsating button.

Kay plunged into the abyss as soon as she felt the probing of Joanne's tongue in her hole. She could never have dared hope for this kind of enthusiasm in her young co-worker, and she delighted in Joanne's unbridled sensuality. She came with a force she had not known in years. Even with the most experienced of lesbians, Kay could not remember feeling the sheer deliciousness of pleasure that Joanne had given her. It was this thought that lingered in her mind as collapsed in a daze between Joanne's thighs and joined the younger woman in sated slumber.

* * *

Matteo Borgas was very proud of his costume as he marched along with the *Escola* Corcovado. But he was prouder still of his young wife's, for yesterday afternoon he had taken her to the Trocadero Hotel to be interviewed by Diego Silva, the magnetic forty-five year old manager of the restaurant. Diego had been in a very vile mood, because he had heard from one of his waiters that his assistant manager Francisco da Rucosta was quitting and taking a job in Sao Paulo without so much as a by-your-leave or even a week's notice. Diego was inclined to ulcers, because he prided himself in running the best restaurant along the beach in Rio, and this loss of his right-hand aide irked him greatly. But worst of all, one of his waitresses had just quit to get married, having been romantically proposed to on Friday night, the very eve of the Carnival, which left him short-handed when patrons were demanding extra service and especially imaginative meals.

Matteo Borgas hadn't thought of trying to get Luisa a job where he worked, at the Hotel del Lorca, because he knew that old Esteban Campos, the hotel's assistant manager, was a bottom-pincher and a rogue who expected to get pussy for nothing from a girl just for the favor of not discharging her. Diego Silva was another matter. Diego was already married to a very shrewish wife, from whom he was separated, and he was known as a man who would pay for his pleasures. Matteo had been told this by one of his friends in the *escola*, and, acting on a hunch, he had gone over that very afternoon with Luise in her prettiest dress.

Diego Silva had beamed when he saw the lovely, full-breasted young wife of Matteo Borgas, and his eyes had lingered on the thick braid that fell to the middle of her back and which was glossy in its silken beauty. Luise blushed demurely and lowered her eyes as a humble and well-trained wife ought to do when in the presence of superiors. Matteo, his hat in his hand, remarked that Luise was herself an exceptional cook, and that she could make the finest feijoada in all Rio. Besides which, he rhapsodically insisted, she made the humblest hovel a palace, and the way she served a man would make him feel like a king even if he were only a poor field hand.

Diego Silva was impressed. Without further ado, he hired Luise on the spot. Then, since he was a blunt man, and given to candor, he looked steadily at Matteo Borgas and said. "You are aware that this is Carnival, *Senhor* Borgas?"

"But of course, estimable manager," Matteo Borgas fawningly replied as he bent his head in acknowledgement.

"Then you must also be aware, as a true *Carioca*, that during our glorious festival, all rules of conduct and morality are suspended, and a stranger may look at a goddess and lust for her."

"That is one of the magnificent facts of our existence, estimable one," Matteo Borgas eagerly agreed. His cunning peasant mind knew at once that Diego Silva wanted to fuck his wife, and he gave Luise a sharp glance and a nod to indicate to her that whatever transaction he might arrange with this personable potentate must necessarily be thoroughly acceptable to her, who had but to obey and honor his commands.

Passion In Rio

"I find your wife excitingly attractive, *Senhor* Borgas," Diego Silva continued. "So much so, that I would be willing to give you the sum of one hundred American dollars, either in dollars or *cruzeiros*, whichever you prefer, if you would leave her here with me during the evenings while the Carnival is in progress, so that I might better explain to her what her many duties will be. It may be that I shall find her worthy of quick promotion and she may even become a salad girl in the kitchen, which in one of Rio's best, as you undoubtedly know."

"It would be a great honor for us both, worthy *Senhor* Silva." Matteo Borgas could hardly conceal his glee. "Luise, you are indeed fortunate to have won the favor of such a fine and gracious gentleman." Then, turning to the genial restaurant manager, he added in a wheedling tone, "I ask only one favor, *Senhor* Silva. I do wish my wife to march with me in the parade of the *escolas* Sunday night."

"So long as she returns here by midnight, I have not the least objection," was Diego Silva's smiling answer.

And thus it was agreed. For seventy-five dollars, Matteo Borgas bought himself a resplendent costume, that of a gladiator, with helmet and trident and fishing net and a papier mache breastplate that looked like genuine silver. As he strutted down the street and glanced at the admiring spectators on each side, he spied a petite olive-skinned young woman with dazzling golden hair, wearing what seemed to be nothing more than a shift, so gauzy was it and so lasciviously did it cling to her jutting breasts and her lusciously rounded bottom. On impulse, he moved over to the left side of the street and saluted her with his trident. She blew him a kiss, and Matteo Borgas called out. *"Tem compromisso para esta noite?"*

He saw the girl smile and nod, and then heard her

husky voice call out with the most thrilling note of eagerness. "Oh, yes, *Senhor*, I am free this night indeed. Come ask for Lola at *Numero Seite, Calle de Riojo*."

"Do not accept any other *Carioca* but myself, beloved lLola," he cried, and then continued his strutting down the street with the members of his *escola*.

At this very moment, his beautiful young wife was naked, except for her long thick braid of black hair and her sandals, and she was lying on the couch in the private suite, which Diego Silva had engaged for himself to celebrate this good fortune of finding a maid, a potential assistant cook, and a delectable mistress, all rolled into one for wages that would not exceed more than a thousand *cruzeiros* a week, the sum he would have had to pay for just a good waitress.

Luisa's eyes were big and round with admiration as she stared at his massive prick. He stood with hands on hips facing her, vainly proud of his manhood. Luise blushed properly, as befitted a bride who had not had any other man but Matteo since their wedding night—though this was only because of circumstance. In the *favela* where they lived, she had seen many a lusty fellow whose bulging fly filled her with a churning desire to be fucked, and the thought of being fucked by someone besides Matteo was a very naughty and exciting one. Now she could hardly wait, knowing that Matteo had given his consent to what was going to happen to her. She had promised herself to do everything that would be required of her to hold this job, for now they would have much more money for their house, to load their table with the fine food her dear Matteo so loved, and to buy an occasional dress and even a pair of fine nylon stockings, which she had always coveted.

"Oh my, *Senhor* Silva, it is so tremendous that I am afraid." She put on a little-girl mien as she stared at his bludgeon of lust. "It will never go in, I am certain."

Passion In Rio

"I am not of your opinion, my beautiful one," he chuckled. "But let us at least make the trial attempt."

"Willingly, *Senhor*," Luise politely murmured. She spread her thighs as wide as she could, and she held out her arms to him. Diego Silva mounted the couch, and allowed Luise to fondle his thick, plum-headed prick between her soft palms, grinding his teeth and snorting to indicate that she stirred him mightily, but that he was still master of his own destiny and in control.

When at last the tip of his mighty organ was introduced between the soft pouting pink lips of Luise Borgas' pussy, she uttered a moaning little sigh of delight and gasped out, "Oh, *Senhor* Silva, be quick, do be quick, I am dying for it! Hurry and let me find out if it will go all the way into me!"

It did, and in a way that caused Luise Borgas unspeakable ecstasy. It was almost like being with Matteo, but better because it was illicit. *Senhor* Silva rammed that huge cock into her deep and far.

"Oh, give it to me boss man," came Luise's cry.

"Don't worry, baby, now that you're working for me, you're going to get to know this fat prick real good."

"Oh, please give it to me. Make me happy with your monster cock. Fuck me hard."

"You're going to be a good little worker, aren't you?"

"Oh, yes. I'll do anything you want me to."

"Well, that's my girl."

With this, Diego Silva pushed his prick up the young juicy cunt one more time, as deep as it would go. The groans that emanated from both parties signaled that this final friction against Luise's love button was enough to send her thighs shuddering. As his partner's head jerked back in pleasure Diego Silva shot his load into the slick love canal.

As her breathing returned to normal in the aftermath of furious orgasm, Luise Borgas thought to herself what a lucky young woman she was, to live in Rio, to have such a wonderful new job, and to have such an understanding and capable boss. And also what a good husband she had, for if Matteo Borgas had not consented, it would have been very taxing on her nerves to have said no to a man with so monstrously huge and vigorous a cock.

When Matteo Borgas and his companions finished their parade and went into a tavern to drink *cachaca*, he excused himself and slipped away. Fortunately the address of the delicious, petite Lola was within walking distance, for you couldn't get a cab for love or money now. The cab drivers themselves were celebrating the Carnival. He found himself before the door of an elegant apartment building with five stories. Then he scowled, because he didn't know Lola's last name, nor what room she lived in. As he stood there in the lobby staring blankly at the nameplates, the grizzled old janitor came out, wearing the costume of a fireman and blowing a long red horn such as one finds on the tables of elegant restaurants on New Year's Eve.

"A happy Carnival to you, *Senhor!*" the old janitor bleated in a voice that was rather sodden with too much rum. "May I be of service? For which of my illustrious tenants are you looking?"

"I met a delightful young woman who called herself Lola and who told me that she lived here, my good friend," was Matteo Borgas' reply.

"Ah, that one! The last name is Orandez. But she has someone with her at the moment. A very wealthy norteamericano, I think. Still, she'd be very angry with me if I drove you away. Perhaps you would wait until the gentleman is finished. Then I am sure she will want to do business with you."

"Business?" Matteo blankly echoed.

Passion In Rio

"But of course, *Senhor*! Lola is one of the wealthiest prostitutes in all our beautiful city. She has men panting after her night and day, and sometimes there are not enough hours to accept all the suitors who wish to pay her."

"Pay?" Matteo Borgas again echoed. Then he clapped his hand to his head and swore an unprintable oath. "On Carnival, I, Matteo Borgas, to pay to fuck a woman? Let me be exiled to Tierra del Fuego instead! I bid you a happy Carnival yourself, old man!"

And with this, grumbling to himself, the husband of young Luise Borgas flung open the door of the lobby and disappeared into the street. He was going to get very drunk tonight.

-14-

Roger Porter had left his wife Lucille in their suite at the Hotel Metropole this Sunday, and told her that he wanted to be by himself for a few hours so that he could think things over. Lucille, her eyes red and swollen from constant weeping, didn't even reply as she watched him close the door behind him. It was over. The idea of a second honeymoon hadn't worked out at all. And yet if only he had tried to understand, tried to be more compassionate. It was only that Roger was so brusque, so matter-of-fact, treating her as if she were simply a receptacle for his hard prick whenever he needed to get his rocks off, and not a woman with emotions that had to be wakened.

She had been so distracted by the shattering knowledge that they had come here, thousands of miles from New York, only to reach an abysmal ending of their union that she hadn't heard him say, "I'll send you up a bite to eat, Lucille. He knew that she liked an omelette and a tossed salad and a little white wine. So he stopped downstairs at the restaurant, gave the order and suggested that it be sent up half an hour later. As he turned to leave the hotel, he encountered handsome young Renaldo Vaneiros, who had celebrated his birthday yesterday, the first day of the Carnival, and who, much to his own sorrow, had been summoned back to work today with the promise that he could be off Monday and Tuesday for the rest of the festival.

Passion In Rio

Renaldo wasn't especially happy for another excellent reason. He had had a quarrel on Friday night with Eleanora Gonsalves and he had blurted out that perhaps they ought to call it off because he was getting tired of her. It had been a very unfortunate thing to say, because Eleanora had just discovered that she was pregnant and she was quite certain that Renaldo was the father. He had denied it angrily, and she had slapped his face and told him to go to the devil, saying that she was going to marry Jose Verduga, who ran a bicycle shop near the Museum of Fine Arts.

What he didn't know was that Eleanora wasn't pregnant at all but had decided to try that as a last trump card to snare this handsome Brazilian who had such an excellent job at the hotel. Also, she liked the way he fucked her and especially the way he would run his tongue lingeringly along the tender moist satiny surface of her inner thigh. In fact, she preferred this to being fucked, though she had never dared to tell him that for fear he might think her somewhat perverse. But whenever he did it to her before inserting his manly organ, Eleanora experienced the most violent orgasm she had ever known, and so she tried as ingeniously as she could, whenever they were together, to get him to lick her legs and even her pussy, which she shaved and to which she applied a very delicate floral perfume.

Renaldo was beginning to worry this afternoon about what he was going to miss when Eleanora wasn't always at his beck and call. She was really a handsome bitch, no two ways about it, and she really was cooperative. He had fucked a great many girls, ever since he was thirteen to be exact, but never one who could twist and wriggle and bite and claw under him the way Eleanora did. Maybe it had been a great mistake to tell her that he had been looking for another piece of pussy, he reflected. And so when Roger Porter, recognizing him as the bellboy who had brought up their bags when they had come in from the airport, smiled at him and nodded, Renaldo graciously returned the smile and inquired after the *Senhor*'s health. As Roger Porter walked down the steps to summon a taxi, Renaldo remembered that the norteamericano had a very delicious wife with red hair and green eyes. He wondered idly how good she was in bed and why the *Senhor* would go off without her. Then he shrugged. It really wasn't any of his business.

He was next in line when the assistant manager of the restaurant came out into the lobby looking for a bellboy, and the one ahead of him had just been summoned by the desk clerk. Renaldo inclined his head at the assistant manager's gesture and hurried forward. "You'll take this tray to *Senhora* Porter and be quick about it. Her husband said it was to be delivered in exactly half an hour and that's just the time. Don't keep her waiting. They are very honored guests, and they have one of our best suites," the assistant manager scolded.

Renaldo made a face, which of course wasn't seen by the officious restaurant man, took the tray and got into the elevator.

A few moments later he tapped discreetly at Lucille Porter's door. A few moments later, still without a reply from within, he put one hand to the knob of the door and turned it. It swung open, and since he had been impressed with the need for delivering the *Senhora* Porter's order, he went slowly into the living room and set the tray down on the table near the couch.

There wasn't a sound anywhere. Wait a minute—what was that? It sounded like someone crying. Renaldo moved forward with a sinuous and almost feline grace towards the hall connecting with the bedroom. The sound grew louder. There was no doubt about it, some-

Passion In Rio

one was crying. When he reached the bedroom door, he found it open. He took one step forward and remained thunderstruck, his mouth agape.

Red-haired Lucille Porter lay on her bed, an arm over her face, naked as Venus emerging from the waves. Her left hand covered her pussy but it wasn't motionless at all; he could see that one of her fingers was diligently frigging herself, and that she was arching her bare bottom from the bed in a weaving movement that suggested carnal excitement in the most unmistakable way.

Renaldo Vaneiros stood transfixed by what he saw. Lucille Porter couldn't see him, because in the first place her face was turned away from him towards the window and in the second place her arm was over her eyes. But the bellboy feasted his eyes on the dark red tufts of pussy-curls clustering over her mount, at the high perched, tightly spaced, canteloupe-like breasts with their dark coral nipples and their brownish orange aureola. Her willowy body, the long slender thighs and the sleek ripplingly muscled calves, excited him enormously. He felt his cock stirring against his fly, and suddenly his misery at losing Eleanora, together with the uninhibited spirit of Carnival which was pervading the entire city, made him commit an impulsive act which, though he had no way of knowing, was destined to change the life of Lucille Porter, as well as that of her husband.

With a stifled groan, he hurried toward the bed, grasped her thighs with his slim artistic fingers, and buried his face in the fragrant muff of her cunt. Lucille Porter uttered a cry of consternation mingled with sensual delight, without taking her arm from her eyes. She cried out, "Oh Roger, oh Roger, I'm so glad you've come back and you're forgiving me! Yes, do that, oh yes, darling, do me there that way! Lick my lips and tease me with your tongue! Oh! Yes! That's so good!"

Renaldo Vaneiros thought he had stopped breathing. The moment he had begun his impulsive act, he knew with a fatal and sinking heart that this could mean his job and even prison for him. Yet the temptation of Lucille's straddled thighs had been too much for him. But when he heard the husky, tear-choked voice, he pressed his lips fiercely against Lucille Porter's cunt, and began to kiss it. His tongue flicked the rims of her vulva while the naked woman writhed and squirmed, offering up her loins. The fragrance of her cunt emanated to him like a potent love potion, making him giddy with longing. His stiff cock strained savagely against the fly of his trousers, and now he dug his tongue between the twitching, moist and cream-saturated petals of Lucille Porter's pussy.

As he touched her clitoris, the young woman uttered a scream of maddened ecstasy, and flung her arm to one side and opened her eyes. Then she uttered another cry, this one of absolute stupefaction and shame: "Ohhhh my God—what are you doing—who—who—who are you?"

But Renaldo Vaneiros rightly believed that there was no need to reply, for he had already tasted the mercurial longing in Lucille Porter's quim. His tongue dug deeply back again, rubbing the nodule of her love button back into the cowl of protective pussy-flesh, and the naked redhead clenched her fists and pressed them against her mouth, twisting away her face, scarlet with emotion, as she felt herself drawn inexorably along the pathway to the precipice of passion. All she could think of was that her life was waiting, that in the most wonderful way her emotions were being distilled deep within her innermost recesses, and that she had never felt so alive and sensuously aware of her body as a female. His hands on her thighs were strangely gentle, though they gripped the columns possessively. But most of all, the intensity and concentration with which he attacked the amorous path and the startling effect which he procured for her completely obliterated any other conscious desires. She wanted only to come, to feel herself burst forth with all the pent-up lusts that Roger Porter had denied within her being.

And that was why Lucille Porter began to twist and weave her naked hips in the most salacious manner, arching herself spasmodically to mash her cunt against his mouth and nose and to take all the magical attunement that he meant to give.

"Oh God—yes, yes—don't stop—oh my God, it's wonderful—oh it's so good—I don't know who you are, but oh don't stop, please don't stop!" she moaned.

His tongue flattened her clitoris, now let it spring up, rigid and throbbing with excitement. Lucille Porter felt herself almost fainting with the delirious frenzy that churned within her womb. "Take me, take me," she panted, holding out her arms, drawing up her knees in the air and spreading them vastly apart, gaping the moist glistening palpitating lips of her cunt in the most abandoned way. Renaldo Vaneiros needed no second invitation. He rose, his face contorted and crimson with lust. Jerking down the zipper of his trousers, he bared a sizeable organ, elongated and with the meatus separated from the shaft by a narrow circumcisional groove. Kneeling between her straddled legs, he planted his palms on either side of her wriggling hips, staring at her face, at her panting breasts, and then slowly approached his ramrod towards the gates of bliss. Tantalizingly he rubbed his cocktip over the rims of those gaping petals, until it was wet and slick with the saliva he himself put there, and the sweet sensation which he evoked thereby made Lucille Porter almost hysterical with rapture. She was whispering and sobbing and now her fingers clawed the sheets as her head turned from side to side, her eyes dilated and filled with an uncontrollable and unquenchable desire.

"Fuck me! Oh my God, give it to me! Don't make me wait like this, I need it so! Fuck me, fuck me, please!" she cried.

Renaldo Vaneiros slowly impaled her to the very hilt. As she felt his hard turgid weapon thrust deep into her channel, Lucille Porter held out her arms to him in a frenzy again, and this time he accepted joyously. He fell upon her, and her legs at once closed upon his buttocks as she surrendered herself to him with a fervor that she had never known before with a man.

His mouth came down on hers, and she could taste her own secret love juices, and it was thrilling for her, too. He fucked her with slow digging thrusts, drawing back gradually to the very brink only to thrust again. She was whimpering and sobbing, laughing and crying, in the throes of an overpowering crescendo which was building steadily and inevitably in her body. And as he sensed this he quickened his rhythm, and suddenly her nails clawed at him, and her teeth sank into his neck as she gave up all her damned-up love flow.

And thus it was that Lucille Porter, on the second day of the Carnival in Rio, finally passed from a thwarted half-virginal state into passionate and full-blown womanhood.

She made him share the lunch with her, and she kissed him and made a fuss over him and insisted that he take her to watch the parade this evening when his shift was over. She didn't even care if Roger came back and found her with him, she was so ecstatic with what Renaldo Vaneiros had accorded her. But most of all, she was deeply grateful for having discovered in herself the resources whereby she could retain her husband whom she deeply loved. If he only knew how to strike the right chord, what glorious music he could draw from her body's instrument.

Later that night, Lucille Porter and Renaldo

Passion In Rio

Vaneiros stood on the sidewalk watching the parade of the great *escola*s and Renaldo enthusiastically explained to her some of the history of these clubs, the prize for which they strove to outdo each other by means of floats and lavish costumes. As for Roger Porter, he had been watching the parade from about two blocks away on the other side of the street when a pretty teenaged *Carioca* put her arm through his and whispered in broken English, "You want nice girl tonight, *Senhor*? I do everything you like, very cheap. Estrella is clean, the *Senhor* not have to worry."

So Roger Porter had obeyed an impulse all his own, and has gone with the charming black-haired whore. She pointedly told him of her talent for Frenching, and when she led him into her cheap little room, he forgot its squalor when she knelt down before him, opened his fly, took out his cock and began to kiss and fondle it and to lick it. With her on her knees, he shoved his stiff prick down her gullet until her lips felt the wiry scratching of his pubic hair. Nobody had gone down on him in quite some time, so the feelings Roger was experiencing were especially sharp. And he was feeling that he wanted to fuck this whore.

"Ok. On the bed. Now!"

With this command from the handsome *norteamericano*, Estrella knew that she had to obey. From the salty taste of his rod, she could tell that this paragon of virility hadn't gotten it in quite some time. She hopped on the cot, writhing lasciviously for her lover's pleasure, waiting for the handsome knight to enter her kingdom. She licked a finger and began diddling herself while Roger got undressed, watching to see how the hardness of his prick was central to the hardness of his stomach muscles; the tautness in his loins and thighs; the beautiful biceps; the perfect pectorals. "This," she mused, "is something I'm going to enjoy."

"You bet you're gonna like this, honey." With this, Roger lurched forward so his cockhead pried apart the whore's entrance. She gasped as if this were the first time she had been delighted this way.

"Don't worry about me," she advised him, "I can take it anyway you want to give it."

"This is fine, baby, if you can take what I've got to give." As this was the first time in many months Roger had gotten a chance to get off other than giving himself a hand job; it didn't take him long to get where he wanted to be.

"I turn you on, *Senhor*?"

"You bet you do, you little *carioca*. This is great, but it doesn't compare to how you give head." With that, Roger shoved his cock into the whore one last time before exploding.

After Roger's grunts had subsided, and Estrella's own shuddering orgasm was over the young *Carioca* whispered, "The *Senhor* is very passionate. Perhaps it is because he has no wife?"

Roger Porter frowned. "Why do you ask me if I'm married?" he demanded.

The charming young *Carioca* smiled and stroked his hair as she murmured, "Because, *Senhor*, it's plain to see that your wife doesn't do that for you, does she?"

"Certainly not! Let's not talk about my wife, if you please. You're very lovely, and you pleased me very much. Will you let me give you some money?"

Estrella wriggled out of bed and stood with her hands on her hips, a nubile young beauty, her eyes flashing fire. "You don't owe me, *Senhor*. It is true that I do sell my body when I please, but this is the Carnival, and it pleases me to bestow my favor on whomever I choose! If you had wished to be a customer, *Senhor*, I would meet my price. But you see that I did not once mention a single *cruzeiro*!"

Passion In Rio

Roger Porter's face grew contrite as he bent his head. "I beg your pardon. I didn't mean to offend you. Will you forgive me?"

"Now that is better. Let us seal the bargain with a kiss."

He took her in his arms, and his prick renewed its energy as it prodded against her warm furry crotch. As her tongue glided between his lips, Roger Porter felt himself renewed. They went back to bed and it was a memorable time indeed for the New York executive.

When he left Estrella's little room at dawn on Monday, she whispered to him, "It is a very easy secret to learn, *Senhor* Roger. If you will kiss your wife between her legs, you will see how quickly she will learn to kiss you there, and then both of you have great pleasure of each other."

Roger Porter made his way back to the hotel on foot early Monday morning, because he still couldn't find a cab. The streets were strewn with confetti, torn balloons and other Carnival debris. As he crossed the street, he stumbled on something metallic, and glanced down at it. It was an empty cartridge, one of several which Miguel Valdes had fired in the air before the fatal shot which had murdered the husband of his faithless wife's best friend. He lit a cigarette and walked on, marveling at the unequivocal way in which the world's most beautiful city had gone all out for an uninhibited festival and wishing that he possessed the spiritual outlook which would allow him to cast aside all regrets and worries, all hopes and dreams, for so short a time back in New York and be simply a creature of instinct and impulse. He was dog-tired when he got back to the suite. He took a warm shower and then lay down on the bed and was soon fast asleep. And while he slept, he began to dream. He dreamed that he was a sultan, high in a tower on some beautiful mountain overlooking valleys and ocean, and that unbidden, out of a great love for him, the humblest of his many lovely slaves stole into his room and gently and reverently began to caress and to touch him with her lips and tongue and fingers. And in his joy at such devotion, he dreamed that he raised her to the rank of favorite and in his magnanimity pardoned those of his slave girls who were under sentence of the whip or the bowstring.

The sensation was powerful. His body vibrated with new energy. He felt himself taut with desire, and he groped for the unknown woman in the dream. His eyes opened, and he uttered a choking cry of incredulity.

For there, kneeling on the bed, her beautiful breasts dangling like ripe fruits, the nipples swollen with desire, was Lucille, her head bowed over his stiff prick which she was gently brushing with her lips and the tip of her pink tongue.

He was speechless. But the throbbing agony in his testicles told him that he was on the verge of a Herculean joy and that nothing must be done to mar this perfect, unexpected, incredible moment.

"Let me do it to you too, darling," he said in a husky voice. Somehow an impulse had come to him, born out of the Carnival and out of his passing fling with an adolescent Rio prostitute.

Lucille blushed and gasped as she felt his hands reach for her cheeks and caress her, and then he grasped her shoulders as she crawled toward him, shaking his head and smiling. "No darling, the other way, get down over me, and keep doing what you were just doing," he instructed.

His hands at last grasped her satiny lithe hips, and he drew down the pink fruit of her cunt to his lips and tongue just as her own quivering warm lips closed over the tip of his straining prick.

Passion In Rio

And thus it was that on the next-to-last day of the Carnival in Rio, Roger and Lucille Porter saved their marriage.

-15-

Lorna Destry was praying that she could die. For some forty-eight hours she had remained in this hideous pillory on the cellar of the home of the man known as *Senhor* Hans Landau. Marguerite Villefranche, who had tortured her almost as cruelly as the man who had engaged her, through the youth she had believed loved her, to "pose for bondage pictures."

After he had flogged her nearly to the blood that first time, he had had Marguerite take a feather to her nipples and her cunt till she was beside herself with mingled pain and longing. Then he had ordered her to beg him to bugger her, and when she had resisted out of fear and shame, he had taken pincers from the wall brazier and begun to tweak the shuddering flesh of her straining naked thighs until at last she had capitulated.

He had taken her brutally, like an animal, without even the palliative of Vaseline. Then, finding her "uncooperative," a phrase he had used so often at the concentration camp, the man who was really Gottfried von Arnheim had taken the whip to her again. This time it had been on her breasts and belly until she had fainted.

When she came to, it was nightfall and she was alone in the cellar, locked in the pillory, her feet arching on tiptoe, her neck and wrists agonizingly chafed by the pitiless clamps of the pillory yokes. Then that hideous man and his red-haired creature had entered the dungeon again, both of them tipsy, and from the slurred

Passion In Rio

remarks which she had heard Marguerite make, Lorna Destry had rightly inferred that her torturess was under the influence of drugs.

With malicious cunning, Gottfried von Arnheim had dosed Marguerite Villefranche's liqueur with a pill containing hashish, together with a tiny pinch of cannabis. It had made the handsome and perverse young Frenchwoman savagely lustful and sadistic. He had sprawled in an armchair, naked except for boots to the knees, boots with those shining silver spurs, puffing at a cigar and chuckling as he watched his naked mistress whip Lorna Destry's thighs and calves and then the insides of her jerking thighs, using a thin switch and ending the flagellation with half a dozen cuts right up into Lorna's sensitive cunt, which made her faint again.

And then Gottfried von Arnheim had risen swiftly from his chair, seized Marguerite and dragged her over to the sawhorse, brutally clubbed her into unconsciousness with his fists when she began to resist and struggle, and bound her down with her wrists and ankles corded to the bases of the legs of the infernal apparatus whose sharp wooden ridge crushed viciously against her own tender pussy.

He had taken a candle and thrust the haft into her rectum, then lighted the wick. Then, taking a flask with contained ammonia, he had passed it under the nostrils of both unconscious naked women and revived them.

Taking a dogwhip down from a hook on the stone wall, Gottfried van Arnheim flogged Marguerite, landing the blows across her lower back with fiendish skill. He had once bet an Oberst that he could kill one of those inferior bitches with a hundred lashes, and he had won his bet, but he was not trying to kill Marguerite or Lorna—at least not for a long while, so long as each could provide him with the abnormal gratifications for which he had hungered all these years of being an outcast from the defeated and destroyed Third Reich. Then he had taken the red-hot pincers to Marguerite's shoulders and arms, while she shrieked and pleaded with him for mercy. His only answer had been a hoarse laugh and an epithet in German which she did not understand but which consigned her to the lowest order of whores and relegated her to the doomed status of women of the "inferior races" who had been sent to die hideously when he had been commandant of the Nazi concentration camp.

When the burning wick reached Marguerite's distended anus, she writhed and twisted and shrieked poignantly for mercy, promising her sadistic lover unheard-of delights if he would only spare her. He stood smoking his cigar, his prick enormous with lust, as he listened. And then he strode over to poor Lorna Destry in the pillory and, drawing up a tall footstool in front of her, seated himself and, clasping her by the buttocks, arched himself up and fucked her, wrenching the muscles of her arms and shoulders as she still stood confined in that hellish pillory.

Marguerite Villefranche had fainted again when the flames of the burning wick scorched her hyper-sensitive anus. This happened at the exact moment that Gottfried von Arnheim spewed his seed deep into Lorna Destry's quaking cunt. He left her and went back to his mistress, blew out the wick and extricated the candle. Then, his penis hard, he sodomized her, leaning over her and reaching under her to squeeze and pinch her panting bubbies, grinding her mercilessly against the infernal sharp ridge of the sawhorse till blood oozed from the lips of her chafed pussy. And again she fainted.

But unbeknownst to Gottfried von Arnheim, a man was ringing the doorbell of his elegant mansion; and his housekeeper, Amelia, answered the summons. She had an idea of what was going on down in the subterranean

Passion In Rio

dungeon, and she loathed and despised her master, though he paid well and at times had gone to bed with her and fulfilled her own lusty nature. But she had sensed somehow that infernal desires whirled in his mad brain and she took pains never to be alone with him and never to go down to the cellar with him.

When she opened the door, a tall gray-haired man, dressed in a rumpled business suit, stood before her. He asked for her master by the name she knew, the *Senhor* Hans Landau.

"He is busy, and cannot be disturbed," Amelia said curtly, and began to close the door. But the man shouldered his way in and, drawing a pistol, went through the house in search of her employer, Amelia following and protesting this intrusion.

"What do you want with the *Senhor* Landau? I will try to find him, though he gave word he was not to be disturbed," she at last said, for she did not like the look of grim determination on the face of the stranger.

"He is a Nazi war criminal," the man replied. "We have finally traced him, though it's taken many years. If you wish to do the world a service, you will tell me where he is. You need have nothing on your conscience, *Senhora*."

Amelia thought quickly. She had heard how Eichmann had been seized in Buenos Aries by members of the Israeli underground. And so *Senhor* Landau was like that one, was he? Well, it didn't surprise her the least little bit. In his safe in the library, there were millions of *cruzeiros*. And she knew the combination. Let this man take the old fool. She would be wealthy beyond her dreams. She shrugged and said calmly, "I'll take you to him, *Senhor*."

She led him down the stairs along the narrow passageway to the metal door through which Lorna Destry had passed. She hammered on the door, and after a few minutes, she heard the turning of the key in the lock from the other side and the door opened. Her employer's bald head stuck out, his face flushed and sweating, livid with lust, a snarl on his lips. "*Vas ist los, du Dirne?*" he growled. "Don't you know I told you I wasn't to be bothered?"

The man in the rumpled suit sprang forward quickly, seized the edge of the door with his left hand and flung it wide. Gottfried von Arnheim uttered a malevolent shriek of rage and fury. The man leveled his gun and pulled the trigger. The ex-Nazi clutched at his chest and crumpled to the floor.

Amelia crossed herself devoutly, shuddering with loathing and terror as she stared down at that gross body. Then her eyes fixed on the sawhorse and on the pillory, and she uttered a cry of compassion. "Oh, *Senhor*, we must free them, he's been torturing them! The monster, the beast, and I never knew!"

But Lorna Destry was inert when the executioner of the Nazi war criminal and Amelia finally unlocked the pillory and lifted her out of its evil yokes. She had succumbed to a heart attack, and perhaps it might be said that she died of love and for love…for the knowledge that her faithless young lover had seduced her only to bring her to this horrible dungeon to be the strumpet-toy of the Nazi beast had crushed her will to live.

And thus after fifteen long years, and in the midst of Rio's great Carnival, one of the most despicable of all war criminals, met a just end and the pitiful life of a Miami waitress was snuffed out at the same time.

* * *

It was Thursday morning and Lent had begun. The Carnival was over. Roger and Lucille Porter were catching the afternoon Pan Am Clipper back to New York, and Roger Porter was very authoritative when he

Passion In Rio

argued with a ticket agent at the airport, insisting that he and his wife have seats together. A little bribe helped arranged this, because there were only two separately placed seats when he had come to arrange his flight back to New York and a new start in marriage. Lucille, her arm tightly wriggled around his, smiled adoringly at him. She was very grateful. But she didn't think she was going to tell him that a Brazilian bellboy at the hotel had taught her how the release her flesh from the stultifying inhibitions which had kept her from being a real wife to her darling Roger. And he, for his part, was hardly going to tell her that he had spent a glorious night with a young Rio prostitute who, oddly enough, had made him a gift of herself because of the Carnival.

* * *

Lawrence Valery and his cousin, Phyllis, were going home together, but their mother had gaily told them that she was going to stay several more weeks, perhaps even longer. She was wiring her husband's good friend, Douglas Arden, the bank executor who handled their estate. Mr. Arden would look after Lawrence and Phyllis until such time as she decided to come back to New York. She needed a vacation. She might even think of opening a little shop down here in Rio. She was a pretty fair designer, and she had always wanted to try her skill with gay colors, such as were seen during the memorable Carnival.

Lawrence and Phyllis didn't mind at all. They had pledged themselves a secret troth, and they were going to be lovers until each of them found a worthy mate. The news that their mother wasn't going back with them didn't sadden them as much as she had expected, but then Alice Valery was too blindly in love with her bellboy lover to worry about how her children felt at the moment.

Joanne Claremont and Kay Arnold were going back on the same plane, too. They weren't hostile any more, and Joanne was wondering if she was going to get married right away to David as she had planned. It would be nice to work on the ideas she and darling Kay had derived from the costumes of the Carnival. And it would be nice to go away from a weekend together to a place like Grossinger's or maybe Saranac. David would always be around and she could always marry him. But she wanted to give free rein to her newfound love, the lesbian Kay Arnold.

***

Miguel Valdes was in jail, awaiting trial. He couldn't understand what had happened and how Miranda had double-crossed him by letting her best friend wear her costume. He only hoped they wouldn't put him to death for murder. But then, a crime of passion would be understandable during the Carnival, when every human emotion is aroused to its zenith and every temptation preys upon the frailties of human flesh.

***

Matteo Borgas and Luise were in bed making love before breakfast on Thursday morning. Matteo wouldn't have a chance that night, because Luise had a date with her new boss Diego Silva. But that was quite all right. The experience Luise was going to get with a fine gentleman like the *Senhor* Silva would make her an even better bed-partner, and she was very good already.

***

Carlos Nuncialto, the bellboy who had led Lorna Destry to what she had believed would be her supreme happiness in life and had resulted in her death instead, was a very unhappy young man on Thursday morning.

He had bought the ticket to the masked ball at the Copacabana Palace for Tianha, and then he had tried to get in touch with her, only to find out that she'd left for Petropolis and would stay at one of the world's finest resort hotels, the Quitandinha, set in the middle of fantastic tropical scenery, including orchid-draped trees on the edge of a small lake. It was near the royal palace built by the last emperor of Brazil, Dom Pedro II. At the ball, she had met a fabulously wealthy importer, twice her age, who had offered her a vicuna coat and a diamond ring to join him for a week as his mistress. Carlos was so surly over the affair, indeed, that by the end of the day he was no longer on the payroll of the hotel.

He thought to himself that he might go find Lorna Destry and make up with her. But by then the afternoon papers printed the story of the assassination of Hans Landau, who had actually been Gottfried von Arnheim, notorious and long-sought war criminal. Also, the story mentioned that a norteamericana had been found dead in the house under suspicious circumstances that smacked of foul play. Carlos decided he would try for a job at one of the smaller hotels in San Paolo, where he could make a fresh start. There would be bound to be rich turista women who would pay him well to service them.

And so everyone who took part in the 1960 Carnival of Rio came away altered in one way or another. The colorful kaleidoscope had come full turn, touching dark lives with brightness, darkening lives that had once been bright. But the pulsing, vital, magnificent city of Rio de Janeiro remained unchanged and timeless.

OTHER BOOKS AVAILABLE FROM MASQUERADE'S EROTIC LIBRARY...

PAUL LITTLE

PASSION IN RIO   54-8 $4.95
"There is a very rich man who is a photographer," he said shifting his eyes nervously, "he wishes to have a North American woman pose for him. He will tie you up and make you wear a costume such as prisoners wore many hundreds of years ago. And for this he will pay a great deal of money. Will you do that?"

LUST OF THE COSSACKS   41-6 $4.95
The carriage stopped in front of the house, and Vassili, who was first to open the door, bowed his head low in homage to his young master, "Welcome, master," he said humbly. Piotr Kalinnikoff, in his resplendent captain's uniform, smiled and turned to Olga: "You see how I'm thought of here my beauty," he chuckled. "You'll have more attention here than at the Czar's own court, and the command performances will be much more exciting!"

LISETTE JOYAUX   10-6 $4.95
An innocent maid, in a quiet village, falls into a nest of lesbians. The four lovely ladies overpower her and explore her. They stimulate every opening in her body, sucking her sweet virginal nectar. To their delight, she returns their caresses with licking lust that excels their own. They have awakened a ferocious lesbian appetite. After she marries, the lusty lesbians kidnap the young bride for some more Sapphic savagery. Fiery French perversions

THE SLAVES OF CAMEROON   49-1 $4.95
This erotic tale of set during the German occupation of Cameroon is about the women who are used by German officers for salacious profit. The woman were forced to become whores for the German army in this African colony. The most perverse forms of erotic gratification are depicted in this classic tale!

THE TEARS OF THE INQUISITION   34-3 $4.95
Even now, in mortal terror, Rosanna's nakedness reminded her of her happily married nights. Even now, there was a tickling inside her as her nervous system reminded her that she was ready for sex. But before her was a man for whom she could feel only the most deeply rooted horror—the Inquisitor!

THE DISCIPLINE OF ODETTE   47-5 $4.95
In turn of the century France, young maidens were threatened with whippings to teach them to protect their virtue. But Odette's family was harsh even for that less enlightened time. Whippings...public humiliation...not even these punishments could keep Odette from Jacques, her lover. She was sure marriage to him would rescue her from her family's "correction." But, to her horror, she discovered that Jacques, too, had been raised on discipline. She had exchanged her father's harsh hand for the more imaginative corrections of a loving husband. Painful pleasures!

THE DELICIOUS DAUGHTER   53-X $4.95
She shivered a little, turned her face to the other side, closed her eyes and continued to wait. The naked skin of her buttocks twitched spasmodically, but other than that she exhibited no signs of apprehension or distress. She knew that her mother would leisurely remove her bathing suit, put on a slip and robe and not come back into her room until the exact moment announced out at the beach. It was usually anywhere from fifteen minutes to a half an hour, and the longer the delay was used when the offense was extremely serious, as apparently it was this time, for the wait became almost interminable.

POOR DARLINGS   33-5 $4.95
Here are the impressions and feelings, the excitement and lust that young women feel when they are first forced into submission. Not just by male partners—but by their aunts and uncles, their step-fathers and their sorority sisters. Desperate, gasping, scandalous sex!

CAPTIVE MAIDENS   12-2 $4.95
Three beautiful young women, whose only sin was to be poor, find themselves powerless against the wealthy, debauched land owners of 1824 England. Their masters force them to do their bidding beneath the bite of the whip. For resisting they are sentenced to imprisonment in a sexual slave colony where they are corrupted into eager participation in every imaginable perversion. Blazing with punishing passion!

THE LUSTFUL TURK   28-9 $4.95
In 1814, Emily Bartow's ship was captured by Tunisian pirates. The innocent young bride, just entering the bloom of womanhood, was picked to be held for ransom—but held in the harem of the Dey of Tunis where she was sexually broken in first by crazed eunuches, corrupted by lesbian slave girls and then given to the Queen as a sexual toy. Turkish Lust unleashed!

TURKISH DELIGHTS   40-8 $4.95
Fazida Kaldos was born in Cario where her father had been an antique dealer. Unhappily, two years ago, he had been brought to the palace, forced to confess his activites to the last iota, and then strangled with a bowstring. Fazida herself had been arrested and brought to the private quarters of Major Eban Hassar, who planned to make her his mistress.

SLAVE ISLAND   19-X $4.95
The good ship *Anastasia* is lured to an uncharted island in the Pacific. The passengers soon learn this is no ordinary speck of land. For Lord Henry Phibrock, a sadistic genius, has built a hidden paradise where captive females are forced into slavery. They are trained to accommodate the most bizarre sexual cravings of the rich, the famous, the pampered and the perverted. Beyond all civilized boundaries!

JOCEYLN JOYCE

THE JAZZ AGE   48-3 $4.95
This is an erotic novel of life in the Roaring Twenties. A Wall Street attorney becomes suspicious of his mistress while his wife has an interlude with a lesbian lover. The Jazz Age is a romp of erotic realism in the heyday of the saxophone and the speakeasy.

KIM'S PASSION   50-5 $4.95
Kim Osmond arrives from India to stay with her aunt Edwardian London. Determined to love women rather than men, Kim begins an affair with the renowned beauty, Lady Enderby. When the lover's quarrel, Kim gives herself to Lord Philby, an old rake who encourages her affairs with her own sex. Before long Kim takes up with Lady Enderby again and they travel the Continent in a series of debauches. When her aunt dies and leaves Kim a fortune, Kim settles in Paris and she quickly becomes a notorious Left Bank lesbian. Nothing is left unsaid in this detailed account of the erotic life of a beautiful English seductress.

KAMA HOURI

ANONYMOUS

"Not since the Kama Sutra has there been such erotic pleasure"...Dr. Pascale Solange

THE YELLOW ROOM

ANONYMOUS

She reached new heights of pleasure with each passionate stroke

The Metamorphosis of LISETTE JOYAUX

...she told herself that she was legally his, she belonged to him, and in the darkness she was even bolder than she had been before.

ANONYMOUS

Captive Maidens

Their masters' greed for power was exceeded only by their lust for young flesh...

ANONYMOUS

THE EDITORS OF PLAYGIRL

PLAYGIRL FANTASIES　　　　　　　　　　　**13-0**　**$4.95**
Here are the best and hottest female fantasies from the Reader Fantasy Forum of Playgirl, the world's only erotic magazine for women. From a passenger who pays her fare in the back seat of a cab, to a sexy surveyor who likes to give construction workers the lay of the land, to a female choreographer who enjoys creating X-rated dances with a variety of perverted partners, these 38 fantasies will drive you wild. They'll turn you on again and again!

THE MASQUERADE READERS

DANGEROUS LESSONS　　　　　　　　　　**32-7**　**$4.95**
Throughout history the lessons of the lash and sexual dominance have been taught by the powerful to their victims. Here are the corrupt priests of the Inquisition, raping their victims at the stake...Lesbians imprisoning helpless maidens...motorcycle gangs and the female motorists they captured. The ultimate in sexual dominance!

LAVENDER ROSE　　　　　　　　　　　　**30-0**　**$4.95**
A classical collection of Lesbian Literature. From the writings of Sappho, the Queen of the women-lovers of ancient Greece, whose debaucheries on her island have remained infamous for all time, to the turn of the century's Black Book of Lesbianism, "Tips to Maidens" to "Crimson Hairs", a recent Lesbian saga, here are the great Lesbian Writings and revelations. Sappho herself would be turned on!

THE EROTIC READER　　　　　　　　　　**11-4**　**$4.95**
A fantastical "pornucopia" of erotic literature. From the Marquis de Sade's "Justine" to the infamous Chinese "Houses Of Joy", where sexual practices beyond Western imagination took place, to the strongest sexual passages from "Fanny Hill" and Frank Harris' "My Life And Loves", here is the cream of "secret", "taboo" literature.

THE EROTIC READER, VOLUME 2　　　　**18-1**　**$4.95**
Here's proof positive that "the old days" held their own in matters of sex. From "Venus School Mistress", who never found a bad boy who was bad enough, to "Forbidden Fruit", the passions of an incestuous family, these sexual sagas will stimulate every appetite.

EASTERN EROTICA

HOUSES OF JOY 51-3 $4.95
A masterpiece of China's splendid erotic literature. This book is based on the *Ching P'ing Mei*, banned many times. Despite its frequent suppression, it somehow managed to survive.

DEVA-DASI 29-7 $4.95
Dedicated to the cult of the Dasis, the sacred women of India who dedicated their lives to the fulfillment of the senses, this book reveals the secret sexual rites of Shiva. It follows the apprenticeship of a young mistress of the Dancing God, showing sexual practices unknown, undiscovered by the West. The secrets of the craft of sex that will set you on Fire! Erotic beyond Western imaginations!

KAMA HOURI 39-4 $4.95
Ann Pemberton, daughter of the British regimental commander in India was kidnapped by her servant in revenge for his whipping. Forced into a harem, Ann was whipped into sexual submission and offered to any warrior who wished to mount her. The whippings kindled a fire within her and Ann, sexually ablaze, became a legend as the white sex-bitch of Indian eroticism!

THE CLASSIC VICTORIAN COLLECTION

A WEEKEND VISIT 59-9 $4.95
Dear Jack, Can you come down for a long weekend visit and amuse three lonely females? I am writing at Mother's suggestion. Do come!

THE YELLOW ROOM 02-5 $4.75
Two complete erotic masterpieces. The "yellow room" holds the secrets of lust, lechery and the lash. There, bare bottomed, spread eagled and open to the world, demure Alice Darvell soon learns to love her lickings from her perverted guardian. Even more exciting is the second torrid tale of hot heiress Rosa Coote and her adventures in punishment and pleasure with her two sexy, sadistic servants, Jane and Jemima. Feverishly erotic!

THE ENGLISH GOVERNESS 43-2 $4.95
When Lord Lovell's son was expelled from his prep school for masturbation, his father hired a governess to tutor the motherless boy—giving her strict instructions not to spare the rod to break him of his bad habits. But governess Harriet Marwood was addicted to domination. The whip was her loving instrument. With it, she taught young Richard Lovell to use the rod in ways he had never dreamed possible. The downward path to perversion!

ANONYMOUS

SACRED PASSIONS   21-1 $4.95
Young Augustus comes into the heavenly sanctuary seeking protection from the enemies of his debt-ridden father. Soon he discovers that the joys of the body far surpass those of the spirit.

THE NUNNERY TALES   20-3 $4.95
Innocent novices are helpless in the hands of corrupt clerics. The Abbess forces her rites of sexual initiation on any maiden who falls into her hands. Father Abelard delivers his penance with smart strokes of the whip on his female penitents' bottoms. After exposure to the Mother Superior and her lustful nuns, sweet Emilie, Louise, and the other novices are sexual novices no longer. Cloistered concubinage!

PLEASURES AND FOLLIES   26-2 $4.95
The Erotikon of an English libertine. "I got astride her, rode her roughshod, plied the crop...Ashamed by these excesses provoked by my reading, I compiled a well-seasoned Erotikon and it excited me to such a degree that I...well, pick up my book, gentle reader, and you'll see whether it has a similar effect upon you."

AUTOBIOGRAPHY OF A FLEA II   07-6 $4.75
The world-famous flea journeys to France where he continues to pen his observations on female sexual foibles from his special vantage points. The buttocks of busty, lusty Dame Lucille. The love nest of luscious soon-to-be-ex-virgin Laurette. And between the breasts of Madame Bernard who longs for the nine inch penance that lies beneath sly Père Mourier's cassock. A real French tickler!

FRUITS OF PASSION   05-X $4.75
A classic study of Victorian sexual obsession. From his initiation into endless orgiastic delights by the slippery lips of the chambermaid sisters, Rose and Manette, the Count de Leon continues his erotic diary for forty years, ending with his Caribbean voyages with the two most uninhibited Victorian Venuses he has ever known. A life totally dedicated to sex!

THE EROTIC READER

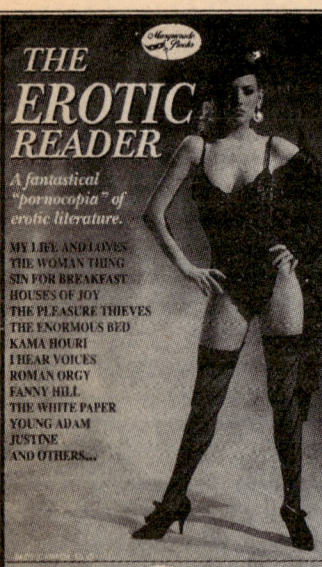

A fantastical "pornocopia" of erotic literature.

MY LIFE AND LOVES
THE WOMAN THING
SIN FOR BREAKFAST
HOUSES OF JOY
THE PLEASURE THIEVES
THE ENORMOUS BED
KAMA HOURI
I HEAR VOICES
ROMAN ORGY
FANNY HILL
THE WHITE PAPER
YOUNG ADAM
JUSTINE
AND OTHERS...

The Lustful Turk

She grew to love her captor and the unspeakable indignities he forced upon her

ANONYMOUS

$4.95 (CANADA) $5.95

Deva-Dasi

"Do not be afraid little handmaid of Shiva. You have surely been taught that love is one of the most sacred delights."

ANONYMOUS

$4.95 (CANADA) $5.95

POOR DARLINGS

He said he would like me to pretend I was his little slave-girl

Title	Code	Price
THE MEMOIRS OF MADELEINE	01-7	$4.75
SECRETS OF THE CITY	03-3	$4.75
LOVE'S ILLUSION	06-8	$4.75
ANNABEL FANE	08-4	$4.75
FRUITS OF PASSION	05-X	$4.75
THE FURTHER ADVENTURES OF MADELEINE	04-1	$4.75
PAULINE	09-2	$4.95
THE METAMORPHOSIS OF LISETTE JOYAUX	10-6	$4.75
THE YELLOW ROOM	02-5	$4.75
AUTOBIOGRAPHY OF A FLEA II	07-6	$4.75
MAN WITH A MAID	15-7	$4.75
PLAYGIRL FANTASIES	13-0	$4.75
CAPTIVE MAIDENS	12-2	$4.95
THE EROTIC READER	11-4	$4.95
EVELINE	14-9	$4.95
SLAVE ISLAND	19-X	$4.95
THE EROTIC READER VOL 2	18-1	$4.95
DARLING/INNOCENCE	24-6	$4.95
THE PRODIGAL VIRGIN	23-8	$4.95
THE GILDED LILY	25-4	$4.95
PLEASURES AND FOLLIES	26-2	$4.95
STUDENTS OF PASSION	22-X	$4.95
THE STORY OF HOLLYWOOD O	16-5	$4.95
THE MISFORTUNES OF MARY	27-0	$4.95
THE NUNNERY TALES	20-3	$4.95
THE LUSTFUL TURK	28-9	$4.95
DEVA-DASI	29-7	$4.95
THE STORY OF MONIQUE	42-4	$4.95
THE ENGLISH GOVERNESS	43-2	$4.95
POOR DARLINGS	33-5	$4.95
DANGEROUS LESSONS	32-7	$4.95
DANCE HALL GIRLS	44-0	$4.95
LAVENDER ROSE	30-0	$4.95
KAMA HOURI	39-4	$4.95
THONGS	46-7	$4.95
THE PLEASURE THIEVES	36-X	$4.95
THE TEARS OF THE INQUISITION	34-3	$4.95
SACRED PASSIONS	21-1	$4.95
THE DISCIPLINE OF ODETTE	47-5	$4.95
THE CARNAL DAYS OF HELEN SEFERIS	35-1	$4.95
LUST OF THE COSSACKS	41-6	$4.95
THE DELICIOUS DAUGHTER	53-X	$4.95
THE JAZZ AGE	48-3	$4.95
THE SLAVES OF CAMEROON	49-1	$4.95
HOUSES OF JOY	51-3	$4.95
MY LIFE AND LOVES (THE LOST VOLUME)	52-1	$4.95
PASSION IN RIO	54-8	$4.95
RAWHIDE LUST	55-6	$4.95
LUSTY LESSONS	31-9	$4.95

ORDERING IS EASY!

MC/VISA ORDERS CAN BE PLACED BY CALLING OUR TOLL-FREE NUMBER

1-800-458-9640

OR MAIL THE COUPON BELOW TO:
MASQUERADE BOOKS
801 SECOND AVE.,
NEW YORK, N.Y. 10017

QTY	TITLE	No.	PRICE
	SUBTOTAL		
	POSTAGE and HANDLING		
	TOTAL		

Add $1.00 Postage and Handling for first book and .50 cents for each additional book. outside the U.S. add $2.00 for first book, $1.00 for each additional book, New York state residents add 81/4% sales tax.

NAME _____

ADDRESS _____ APT # _____

CITY _____ STATE _____ ZIP _____

TEL ( ) _____

PAYMENT: ☐ CHECK   ☐ MONEY ORDER   ☐ VISA   ☐ MC   ☐ AMEX

CARD NO. _____ EXP. DATE _____

PLEASE ALLOW 4-6 WEEKS DELIVERY. NO C.O.D. ORDERS. PLEASE MAKE ALL CHECKS PAYABLE TO MASQUERADE BOOKS. PAYABLE IN U.S. CURRENCY ONLY.

FORM 54-8